D0341657

# Everything's Changed

## Julie Sternberg
### illustrated by Johanna Wright

bmp
Boyds Mills Press    An Imprint of Highlights    Honesdale, Pennsylvania

Boyds Mills Press
An Imprint of Highlights
815 Church Street
Honesdale, Pennsylvania 18431
Printed in the United States of America
ISBN: 978-1-62979-672-7 (print)
ISBN: 978-1-62979-798-4 (e-book)
Library of Congress Control Number: 2016951380
First edition
The text of this book is set in Zemke Hand ITC Std.
The illustrations are done in pen and ink.
Production by Sue Cole
10 9 8 7 6 5 4 3 2 1

For Alyssa, Caroline, and Jackie.
Thank goodness for all of you.
—JS


For Anika Fern
—JW

Do not even think about opening this journal. You don't get to read it. Or touch it.

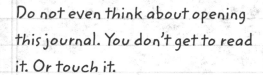

# It is PRIVATE.

You're not special just because you're my big sister, Jo. If you read this, I will find the picture I took when you had that giant pimple on your chin, and I will make copies, and I will tape them up in the hallway of our new school. Where everyone in your grade can see.

Don't assume
I won't do it.
Because I will.

Celie

Dearest Celie,

I'm crossing my fingers that you'll like this new diary. I went through shelf after shelf of journals in the bookstore, trying to find just the right one. I rejected a million (roughly speaking). They seemed too businesslike, or too brown, or too dainty, or too babyish, or too filled with supposedly inspirational sayings like "Find the magic to make your spirit fly."

I found no such magic, but I did finally find this journal. It strikes me as artistic and bold, and those qualities remind me of you. So I bought it.

I hope it feels like the right choice to you. And I hope it helps you make your way through the days we face ahead. I know it'll be hard to move to a new home and a new school, and to have to worry about making new friends. But changes aren't <u>only</u> bad; they can be exciting, too. I know we'll have happy moments as well as challenging ones, and I hope it's helpful to you to describe them all here.

With lots of love, and
then a whole lot more,

Mom

Once upon a time,

this diary became

the very

**private**

**property**

of

<u>Celie Valentine Altman</u>

And so it remains,

to this very day.

The End.

## Sunday, January 30, first day after rotten move

I just wrote a letter to Lula, but I can't mail it. Because the stamps are buried in an unpacked box somewhere. And Mom won't help me find them. She's too busy unwrapping glasses and plates from packing paper and setting them on shelves. She keeps saying, "The kitchen is my priority right now."

Dad won't stop trying to fix a funny smell coming from the dryer. I guess that's his priority.

I need them to make stamps their priority. And also, our Internet and phone! They HAVE to get set up! I can't get in touch with my friends! I feel like a cave person!

me hunt for meat

me miss email

I need help hanging stuff, too. I've got stacks of pants and sweaters and long-sleeved shirts and sweatshirts to hang. They don't fit in my new dresser, which is tiny. Because my room is tiny.

One good thing about this room, though—it's ALL MINE! For the first time in my whole life I'm not sharing a room with Sloppy Jo!

In my very own room, I will never have to worry about Jo setting her wet towels on my bed or spilling nail polish on my desk or leaving bowls of half-eaten, moldy strawberries in my closet. That's one hundred percent good news.

But it can get lonely in here without Jo. I didn't like being all alone last night, when there were shadows and creakings inside this new place, plus sirens sometimes outside, getting closer and closer and louder and louder before fading away.

I'm going to find Jo now. Maybe she'll help me hang my clothes.

## Later

I think Mom might be going bonkers. I just saw her sitting on the floor in the living room, unpacking a box full of photo albums. I asked if she could FINALLY find a stamp for me. It's been HOURS since I asked her the first time.

She didn't answer at first. Instead she looked around
her at all the boxes and bubble wrap and half-filled
garbage bags, plus the stacks of books and folders and
games and binders that haven't been put away yet.

"Why wouldn't I be able to find a stamp?" she said,
after she'd glanced at all of that.

Then she said, "How about a teeny, tiny button?
Would you like a teeny, tiny button, too?"

Then she started laughing. And she DID NOT STOP.
She leaned back and put her hand on her chest and
laughed and laughed and wiped tears from her eyes
and laughed some more.

I should've been annoyed. Because I really need a
stamp, and she was making fun of me! But all that
laughing was contagious. I had to laugh some, too.

I left her on the floor in there, shaking her head
and grinning. And now I'm taping my entire letter to

Lula in here. Since I'm obviously not getting a stamp any time soon.

Dear Lula,

I miss you so much already. I can't believe I'm starting a new school tomorrow, without you and Violet. I don't want to go! I'm not going to know a single person.

Mom and Dad keep saying, "You'll make friends! You'll see!" But they can't know that, right? What if all the kids in my class have bad breath?

We never brush our teeth!

Or what if <u>I</u> mess up? What if I sneeze one of those wet sneezes in class, for example, and I don't cover my face fast enough, and snot and slobber gets on everyone around me? They'll call me "Sneezy" for the rest of my life. And no one will want to get anywhere near me. Not without protective raingear.

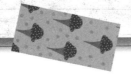

My desk is next to Sneezy's.

The teacher won't let me move.

I know you'd still like me, even if I had a sneezing catastrophe. I wish I could come see you right now. I can't believe I'd have to walk for FIVE HOURS to get there. Or take two different subway trains for more than an hour. We might as well be in Kentucky.

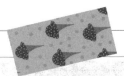

I feel mad at Mom and Dad for moving us so far.
Even though I know their reasons. They've told me
over and over: We needed a bigger place, since
Granny's staying with us and we have to hire a live-
in nurse for her. And they couldn't find a bigger
apartment that we could afford in or near our old
neighborhood. But they should've looked harder!

Jo let me borrow her phone earlier to call you, but
no answer. I'll try again later if she lets me. I wish I
had a phone!

I miss you! Tell Violet hi!
Love,
Celie, who would
like to be doing this:

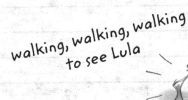

walking, walking, walking
to see Lula

## MUCH LATER

I woke up very worried a little while ago. The clock on my tiny dresser said 2:18 A.M.; I thought I could hear Dad's cell phone ringing; and phones should not ring at 2:18 A.M.

Wrong number? I thought. Or emergency? And then I thought, GRANNY! Because Granny is staying with Cousin Carla until we get settled in our new place. And Cousin Carla could be calling with a Granny emergency.

I threw off my covers and jumped out of bed and ran into the dark hallway. Then BAM! I crashed right into Jo's bike. I banged my side hard, and one of the pedals scraped a chunk of skin off my leg. She needs to move her bike to the basement!

But I ignored the blood and pain and started limping super-fast to Mom and Dad's room. Dad was standing next to his side of the bed with his phone in his hand. Mom was sitting up, watching him.

"You're right," Dad was saying into the phone. "She needs constant, expert care. We'll get everything resolved soon, I promise."

Granny needs constant, expert care.

So I asked loudly, "What is it? What happened? Is Granny okay?"

"Shh," Mom told me. "Let him finish."

Dad kept talking into the phone. "I'm so sorry you have to go through this, Carla," he said. "Thank you for all of the help you give us." He listened to whatever she said. Then he hung up.

"Go through what?" I said. "Tell me."

"Everything is fine," Dad said. "Granny just got a little disoriented and wanted to go outside. So naturally Carla got concerned."

I waited for him to say more. Since that was OBVIOUSLY not all that happened. But he was finished.

"It's two eighteen in the morning!" I told him. "Cousin Carla wouldn't wake us up to say that Granny's disoriented! You're not telling me the whole story."

Dad didn't say I was wrong. But he also wouldn't tell me any more. Instead both he and Mom said things like, "It's late; you have your first day of a new school tomorrow; you need to get some sleep."

Then Dad walked me back to my room. I stopped arguing, since it was obviously not working. I just let him tuck me in. And I listened to him walk back down the hall. Then I grabbed my spy notebook from the drawer in my nightstand and hurried after him as quickly and quietly as I could.

I made it safely past Jo's bike this time. And I stopped right outside Mom and Dad's room. I stood there and listened and wrote this spy report:

# Top-Secret Spy Notebook of

Celie Valentine Altman

**Sometimes spies must move absolutely silently. If you are vigilant about all of your movements, you are less likely to make unnecessary noise while bumping into objects. Practice paying particular attention to the space-time continuum.**

What does that even mean?

I'm paying particular attention to Mom and Dad's voices. They're saying:

Mom: "Why did the doorman stop her?"

Dad: "She was leaving the building in her nightgown. It didn't seem right to him, so he asked her to wait. Then he called up and woke Carla."

Mom: "Thank goodness he was paying attention."

Dad: "I know."

Silence now.

Why are they being so quiet? They need to say more!

**Certain art forms enhance your awareness of, and control over, your own movements. Research dance classes in your area. Make a list of them below.**

This is no time for dance! Mom and Dad are talking again now:

Dad: "Carla feels terrible that she was asleep. She kept saying she never heard Granny leave."

Mom: "It's not her fault."

Dad: "None of this is anyone's fault."

_Another pause._

**Pay attention to the noise that your clothes might make. Sweaty socks can squelch in shoes, for example, and be overheard by your targets.**

_I don't care about sweaty squelching socks._

_Dad again: "Granny told Carla she wanted to see her mother's fern. That's why she left."_

_More silence._

_Mom: "We have to hire a nurse NOW, and we have to get Granny settled here."_

_Dad: "Should we try a different agency? We need a better pool of candidates."_

_Mom: "I'll make calls first thing in the morning."_

I had to hurry back to my room then. Because Dad said, "Did you just hear something? In the hallway?"

I don't think he followed me.

I feel heavy now, with worry. Granny can't go find her mama's fern. That fern is all the way back in Louisiana. Or maybe even dead. But she doesn't understand. I want her to understand.

Plus what if the doorman hadn't stopped her? Granny would've been so shivery and alone, in the middle of this cold night, in a strange neighborhood! She would've gotten lost. She could've gotten frostbite. Or stepped in front of traffic.

I can't think about that for another second. I won't.

I KNEW Granny should've moved here at the exact

same time as us. Even if moving is chaotic, like Mom and Dad kept saying. It's too hard for her mind to go from place to place!

I'll stay up all night tomorrow getting Granny's room ready if I have to. And the rest of this apartment, too. Jo will help. We can't let Granny trip over boxes or bikes. Everything needs to be easy for her.

Also, Mom's right—we have to find a good Stranger Nurse to live with us, and fast. I know she hasn't liked the nurses she's already interviewed, for good reasons. Like the one who asked if she could keep a bat in a cage in her room. Or the one who had the bubbly rash on her hands. It was very hard to look at. Plus what if it was contagious?

I didn't want those people either. Still, we need somebody! Maybe we're being too picky.

Maybe a pet bat wouldn't be so bad?

I'm actually very cuddly.

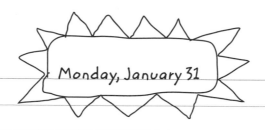

I'm back from school. What a WEIRD day it was!

Jo ended up making us late, because she decided
at the last minute that she HAD to wear her black
and white striped sweater. But she couldn't find
her black and white striped sweater. So she ended
up dumping everything out of seven unpacked
boxes.

THEN, when she'd FINALLY put on the sweater, she
started texting with her very tall boyfriend Jake.
"One more second!" she kept telling Mom and Dad,
who kept saying, "Time to GO!"

I didn't mind all the texting, because Jake passed
on some nice messages for me from his sister Violet,
who's my good friend. Plus I didn't want to get to
the new school. I kept thinking things like, What if I
need to pee and I can't find a bathroom? I wanted
Jo to text forever—I was happy staying home.

But Mom and Dad got more and more annoyed. Finally Mom told Jo, "I am VERY close to throwing that phone in the trash."

Jo stopped texting then, but I said, "I have to pee!" Dad told me, "You were JUST in the bathroom! It's all in your head!" But I refused to leave the apartment until I'd gone again.

After that Mom and Dad rushed us out of our building and up the freezing cold streets of our new neighborhood. Trucks clanged past us, super-loudly. It stank out there, too, because stores had piled up huge garbage bags along the sidewalk.

We have a yummy-smelling bakery about a block from us, though. Walking by there was nice.

Other good things: Our walk to school is short. Only about four blocks. And the school is very interesting looking. It's shaped like this:

We didn't get to look at the building for long, though. Because Dad noticed that there was no one else out there. "I guess the other kids have already gone inside," he said.

Mom looked at her watch and said, "We're a few minutes late."

"Let's just wait until tomorrow," I said.

"No," Dad said. "Today's the first day of a new semester. It's the right time to start."

"It's only the beginning of second semester here because they have that weird intersession," Jo said.

"Plus nobody cares about semesters," I said. "Except you and Mom."

Then a girl and a boy raced past us. The girl had long, dark hair, and the boy had a lot of freckles, and they both looked about my age.

The girl called to the boy, "I'll be in way more trouble than you."

The boy called back, "True. You will." And they both RAN toward the school.

"Come on, Celie," Jo said then. "Let's get this over with."

We told our parents we'd be fine, and we kissed them goodbye. Then we walked into school together.

After we'd opened the heavy fortress door, we saw a security guard, who raised his eyebrows at us. "We're new students," Jo told him. "We just moved here."

Before he could say anything back, someone else cried

out, "Oh! Oh, oh!" and came running at us from inside the school. It was the girl with the long, dark hair.

"I can take one of them!" she said, raising her hand like she was in class. "My dad and I saw Ms. Chanda on the subway yesterday—she told us we're getting someone new in our class. I bet it's you, right?" She pointed at me. "You're in fourth grade?"

I nodded.

"Can I take her?" Dark-Haired Girl asked the security guard, nodding and smiling. "Can I?"

"Fine, Mary Majors," the security guard said. "But you're already late. I want you heading straight to class."

I barely had time to think, What kind of a name is Mary Majors? before she grabbed my arm and started pulling me away.

"Wait—one second," I told her. Because I wanted to say bye to Jo.

But Mary Majors said, "We have to run! Ms. Chanda is going to kill me!"

So we ran down one hall and up two flights of stairs, then down another hall and around a corner. The school felt HUGE! SO MANY MORE classrooms on each floor than at my old school. And louder, too. The halls weren't carpeted, and the sound of our running boomed off all the walls.

One teacher poked her head out of her classroom and called out, "Slow down! Mary Majors Meade, you KNOW not to run in the hallway." So we slowed down.

But not for long! Because Mary Majors glanced back once or twice. And as soon as that teacher had pulled her head back into her classroom, Mary Majors grabbed my arm and started running again.

For two tiny seconds, I didn't let her pull me. Because we'd JUST been told to walk!

But then she said, "Don't worry about Mrs. Haynes. She's too old to follow us. Let's GO!"

She yanked on my arm, and I gave in and ran again. Because I wouldn't know where to go if she left me. And because she was the only kid I knew in my whole grade.

We ran together around a corner and down another long hall, until finally Mary Majors sped through a doorway and stopped short. And I ended up looking like this at the moment I met my new teacher and classmates:

Flying sweat

The teacher had been talking to the class. I don't know whether she even noticed me at first. She just turned and crossed her arms and said, "Mary Majors Meade" in a very disappointed voice.

"I know what you're going to say, Ms. Chanda,"
Mary Majors said quickly. (Somehow SHE wasn't
huffing and puffing and sweaty.) "I know I promised
before break to start being on time. But today
it's not my fault! Because when I got to school, I
overheard the new girl talking to Mr. Manning in
the lobby. And then of course I had to stop and
wait and show her around a little. Because that is
the nice and welcoming thing to do, right?"

I stared at her with my mouth open. She looked
so wide-eyed and ready-to-swear-on-a-Bible
truthful. But she was LYING. To the teacher!

It WAS her fault that she was late. She was
ALREADY late when she heard me talking to the
security guard. Also, she never showed me around
at all! She just made me SPRINT to class, like I was
being chased by a boy who wanted to kiss me.

As I stared at her, not believing her behavior, Mary
Majors did the worst thing of all. She looked at me
and said, "Right, New Girl?"

So I had to decide whether to lie to my teacher or rat out the only kid I'd met in my new class. In front of everyone!

All the kids were watching me like I was the best show they'd ever seen on TV. One red-headed boy looked very worried for me. Like I was just about to step on a porcupine barefoot.

I couldn't figure out what to do. So I smiled at my teacher and made this noise: "Mmnnmmnn." And I prayed she wouldn't ask me to actually say something.

It worked! Ms. Chanda just asked, "Are you Celie?"

I nodded.

"Welcome to class 4C," Ms. Chanda said. "Please take a seat next to Charlie." She pointed at the red-headed boy. "Mary Majors, if you are late again tomorrow, you will get another detention. No excuses."

I sat next to redheaded Charlie, who smiled at me very nicely. And Mary Majors sat far across the room. Which made me happy. I didn't like the lying. Or the running from teachers who told us to walk. Whether or not those teachers were old.

I told myself I could just stay away from Mary Majors. The class was big—much bigger than at my old school.

But about five seconds later, this note landed on my desk:

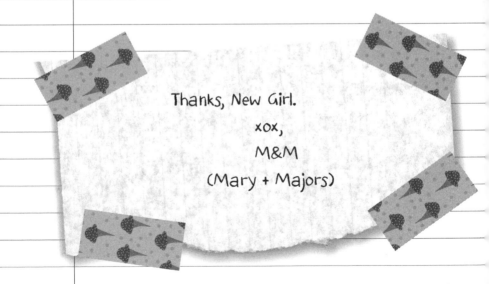

Thanks, New Girl.
xox,
M&M
(Mary + Majors)

I did not send her a note back. Because I had been in class for FIVE MINUTES! I couldn't get caught passing notes that soon! Plus I didn't want her sending me x's and o's. I wanted her to stay away.

But in the cafeteria, at lunch, she rushed over and stood right behind me in the food line. And she said things like "Only get the mac and cheese! The rest will make you vomit." I'd only actually wanted the mac and cheese in the first place. But I got a roll, too. Because I didn't like her bossiness.

Then she said, "Sit here. Right here." And she sat at a table with a couple of other kids at it. And what could I do? Go sit with other kids? I didn't know any of them!

So I sat with Mary Majors. Then other girls started sitting with Mary Majors, too. Asking her how her vacation was, and saying things like, "Listen to what happened to me, Mary Majors!" They were all nice to me, too.

And I felt like maybe I hadn't been fair to Mary Majors before. All these kids definitely liked her. And they'd known her forever. I'd just met her. So maybe I was just being mean.

Plus, after lunch, Mary Majors sent me this note:

See how Andie just asked to go to the bathroom? She had the tacos and corn for lunch. Told you to stick to the mac and cheese!

M&M

I didn't send a note back. Because it was still my first day. But I did turn and smile at her. She waved back.

As I turned around, I noticed that red-headed Charlie was watching me, too. He had a very disappointed look on his face. Like I'd promised that I'd bring him a slice of delicious chocolate cake, but then I'd brought grapefruit instead.

"What?" I wanted to say to him. But I couldn't. Because Ms. Chanda was saying something about annotating our reading assignments, and I had no idea what she was talking about. I had to pay attention.

After the last bell rang, she said I should meet her in the classroom tomorrow morning before school, at 7:30, so she could start helping me get caught up. I have to remember that.

And now I have to go back to doing my math homework, which I took a break from earlier. It is SO HARD. Rates of change problems— EIGHT of them! They're making me feel like this:

# Later—taking ANOTHER Break From VERY HARD math

I just remembered something. Dad owes me big things!

He promised me a popcorn maker, a cotton candy machine, and three beanbags if we moved. Plus an art studio for Granny.

But there's no space in this apartment for an art studio. And my room is too small for a cotton candy machine OR a popcorn maker OR three beanbags.

As soon as he gets home from work, I'm telling him he has to get me other things instead.

Here is what I will accept:

A New Paint Set for Granny

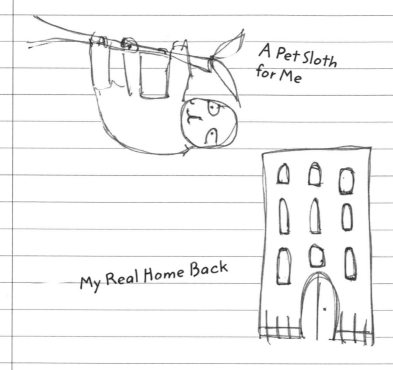

A Pet Sloth for Me

My Real Home Back

## A Little Later

Our doorbell rang about fifteen minutes ago. I knew who was there without even leaving my room. Because Mom had told us that a woman was coming to interview to be our Stranger Nurse.

So I grabbed my spy notebook, and waited for just the right time, and sat in the hall near the living room door. And I listened to that interview.

Here is my spy report:

## From the
# Top-Secret Spy Notebook of
Celie Valentine Altman

**Spies must on occasion travel to foreign lands and appear to be at home. Try acquiring this skill. First, consider how people speak in your foreign land. Research key phrases, like "How much is a first-class ticket?" And, "Yes, I would like to taste the barbecued guinea pig."** _NO, I WOULD NOT LIKE TO TASTE THE BARBECUED GUINEA PIG! I want to warn the poor guinea pig! Stay away from the flames, guinea pig. Stay far away!_

**Research the typical attire of the foreign land. In some nations, for example, it is frowned upon for women to wear shorts, pants, or short skirts. Will you need to change the way you dress?**

_I feel annoyed by those nations. I'm never going to_
_any of them._

_Mom just offered the interviewing Stranger Nurse_
_some cookies, and Stranger Nurse said, "No, thank_
_you." Which is not good. How will we know in time_
_whether she chews with her mouth open? Also,_
_what kind of person doesn't like cookies?_

**Technology might work differently in foreign
lands. You might need a power adapter to
charge a spy camera disguised as a bottle of
hairspray, for example. Are you prepared?**

_I want a spy camera disguised as a bottle of_
_hairspray! I want to walk into rooms and pretend to_
_spray-spray-spray my hair and record everything!_

**Careful planning is critical for every spy.
Make a list of points to consider as you
prepare for your foreign experience.**

<u>Points I am considering:</u>

• This interviewing Stranger Nurse is named Idella Stone. (I think that's how she spells her first name, anyway. She pronounces it Eye-Della.) What kind of a name is that?!

• Eye-Della REALLY likes sayings. For example, after Dad said we'd been through a lot of tough changes recently, Eye-Della said, "Never rains but it pours." And, after Mom asked how long she'd been a nurse where she's working now, Eye-Della said, "Almost ten years, thank the good Lord above. No moss on a rolling stone."

• I don't understand that moss on a stone saying.

• Also, she said this annoying thing: When Mom said, "Granny has been staying with our Cousin Carla for the past several days, as we've been getting settled here," Eye-Della said, "Absence makes the heart grow fonder."

• That was not the right thing to say. Because we CAN'T be fonder of Granny. Her absence doesn't make my heart fonder. It makes my heart sadder.

• Mom told Eye-Della that Granny is coming home on Thursday! Finally! Then Mom asked how quickly Eye-Della could start, if we hired her; and Eye-Della said by the end of the week. So her timing is good. I hope SHE is good! Mom has to figure that out, FAST!

## A Little Later

I'm worried about Jo.

I went to tell her about the Eye-Della interview, and the news about Granny coming home. Plus I wanted to describe the whole Mary Majors situation and ask her advice.

I found her in her new room. Which already has dirty clothes on the floor. Plus books and jewelry and hairbands and wads of mismatched socks all over the top of her dresser.

Sometimes I miss having Jo with me in my room, but I NEVER miss her mess.

Anyway, she was on her bed, watching her phone. And looking sad.

"What's the matter?" I said. "Was school bad?"

"No, school was okay—everyone was really nice," she said. "But Jake was supposed to text me first thing after school to ask me that exact question. He PROMISED he'd do that, because he knew how worried I was, about how it would go. But he still hasn't texted—and I've been trying to get him for hours."

"That's weird," I said. Because even though I never actually wanted Jo to have a boyfriend, I have to admit that Tall Jake is nice.

42

"I know—he's really good about promises, usually," she said. "He always keeps them."

Then Mom called us to dinner. Dad had gotten home, too, and we all talked about the whole Granny coming home/finding a Stranger Nurse situation. Which is a worrying topic.

Plus I felt a little frustrated. Because I wanted to ask Mom, "Why did you tell Eye-Della important information before you told US?" But I couldn't. Because I'm not supposed to spy.

I did feel happy about this, though: It turns out there's a VERY YUMMY pizza delivery restaurant in this neighborhood!

I'm a slice of cheesy goodness.

## A Little Later

AMAZING NEWS!!

Like Hearing
Actual Angels Sing

Dad just came in to check on me. I reminded him that he owes me three beanbags, a popcorn maker, and a cotton candy machine. He said, "Well . . . your mom and I have been thinking about that."

Then he went to get Mom. And they said that since I'm going through so many tough changes, they wanted to give me something they knew I really wanted. And something that will help me keep in touch with my old friends.

44

Then they handed me . . .

MY VERY OWN CELL PHONE!!!!!

It's so beautiful!!

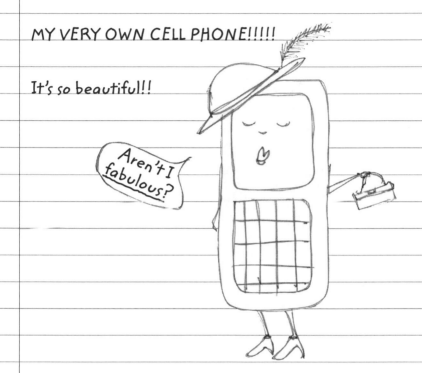

Aren't I fabulous?

I cannot wait for my FABULOUS cell phone to charge, so I can text Lula and Violet. (They both got phones before me. Every single person I know got a phone before me. But that's OK! I have a spectacular one now!)

I wonder what Mom and Dad are giving Jo. Have to go find that out.

# A Tiny Bit Later

Jo got the purple, fuzzy rug she wanted for her room
AND a camera that prints the pictures you take.
(Good gifts, but not as good as my CELL PHONE!)

She was thanking Mom and Dad and smiling and
hugging them when I got to her room. But after
they left, she got even more gloomy than she'd been
before dinner.

"What's the matter?" I asked her. We were both
sitting on her new purple rug, which Dad had put in
just the spot she wanted. I thought maybe she was
mad because she'd had to wait until she was twelve
to get a cell phone. And I'm only ten.

But she shrugged and said, "Jake's being a jerk."

"What do you mean?" I asked.

She shrugged again. Which did not exactly answer
the question.

I pointed to her phone, on her bed, and asked, "Can I see what he said?"

She actually typed in her password then and showed me the texts. Which definitely surprised me. And made me worried. Because Jo does NOT usually like me touching her phone. And she almost never lets me read texts from Jake. I knew if she showed me texts from him now, she must be feeling very bad and needing lots of help. So I paid close attention to everything I read.

Here's what those texts said:

**Jo (about 3:45 PM):** one day down, way too many more to go

**Jo again (about 5:00 PM):** r u home yet?

**Jo again (about 7 PM):** ?

**Now Jake (about five minutes later):** hey

**Jake again:** sorry just texting now. decided to join track. had practice after school

**Jo (about ten minutes later):** ok

**Jake:** coach says i'm pretty fast. won some heats

**Jo:** great

I think maybe Jo was being sarcastic when she texted "great." Because when I stopped reading, she said, "Do you see how he never even asks how my first day was? He just talks about how fast he is. And he doesn't text me at all until AFTER DINNER. Does track go through dinner?"

"It didn't when you were on the team," I said.

"Exactly!" Jo said. "So why did he wait so late to text?"

"You should ask him that," I said.

"No, I shouldn't," Jo said. "Because if I do I'll seem stalker-y."

"Oh," I said. "Okay." Because I don't exactly

understand what's girlfriend behavior and what's stalker-y behavior.

Then I had an idea.

"I'll call Violet!" I said. "She can tell us where Jake was for dinner and why he didn't text you before then."

I liked that idea a lot. But Jo's eyes got big and she started shaking a finger at me.

"DO NOT DO THAT!" she said. "If you tell Violet, then Violet will tell Jake, then Jake will think I've been talking to you about him behind his back, and that you and Violet have been talking about him, and he'll feel weird. Plus he'll think I'm all upset. So DO NOT SAY ANYTHING to Violet. Got it?"

"Got it," I said.

Except, I didn't actually get it. Because Jo IS all upset. And if Jake doesn't know that, he might not fix it. Wouldn't that be bad?

This whole girlfriend-boyfriend thing is very confusing.

## STILL TRYING TO DO THIS MATH!

I cannot look at these math problems ever again. They're impossible! I want to make Ms. Chanda do this problem when I see her tomorrow morning:

"Before today, Celie did 0 rate-of-change math problems. Since coming home from school today, Celie has tried to do 8 rate-of-change problems. Find the rate of increase in the likelihood of Celie's whole entire head exploding."

No more trips to the dentist, at least!

Headless Celie

# Before Bed

I just had my very first texts with Violet and Lula!
I am SO HAPPY to be able to do that!

I was VERY CAREFUL not to ask Violet where Jake
went for dinner. But the subject definitely came up.
I'll copy what we said here:

**Me:** it's CELIE!! mom and dad got me a phone!!!

**Lula:** yyyyyaaaaaaaayyyyyy!!!!

**Violet:** let's text all day every day!!!

**Lula:** was ur new school ok?

**Me:** girl named mary majors being nice.
majors NOT her last name. she gets called
that whole thing—mary majors—all the time

**Lula:** we should call u celie valentine all the
time! or celie ♥

**Violet:** we ♥ celie ♥

**Me:** :-) :-) :-)

**Violet:** hey celie♥, is jo mad at jake?

**Me:** what do you mean?

**Violet:** b/c jake's been trying to text her and she won't answer him

**Me:** oh

**Violet:** is she mad because he went to trina's after track?

**Me:** HE WENT TO TRINA'S AFTER TRACK? WHY DID HE DO THAT? I HATE MEAN-A-TRINA!

**Violet:** i told him not to!

**Lula:** i hate trina, too! remember when we put

hate mail in her locker, celie, b/c she was being mean to jo and that other girl—dee—in their class?

**Me:** yes! I'd already told jo for MONTHS that trina was a terrible person. was so happy when jo FINALLY stopped being her friend

**Lula:** why did jake go to trina's?

**Violet:** idk. he called home after practice and said to tell mom he was going over to a track friend's and he'd be there for dinner, and i said which friend, and he said trina, and I said it seems wrong to go home with girl who's not jo, and he said stop being nosy and just tell mom.

**Lula:** maybe a big group went?

**Violet:** I asked that! just him

**Me:** i have to go tell jo.

**Violet:** k. tell us what happens!

**Lula:** yeah, don't forget!

**Me:** 👍

I did NOT like that Trina news. Because she really is a terrible person, and she doesn't even speak to Jo anymore. Why would she ask Jake to come over??? Definitely not for any good reason.

I hurried back to Jo's room and found her sitting on her bed with a book in her lap. Right away I told her, "Read these texts."

Then I handed her my phone, and I watched her read.

I expected her to turn red-faced and big-eyed. Because that's how she looks when she's mad.

Instead, her face and her shoulders got droopy, and she shook her head.

"What's the matter?" I asked.

"I don't want to talk about it," she said.

"Oh," I said. Then I just stood there, trying to figure out how to get her to talk when she didn't want to.

I guess standing and thinking was a good strategy on my part, because Jo eventually said something. Except, it wasn't something I liked. She said, "I feel so stupid."

"You're not stupid!" I said. "How could you possibly feel stupid?"

"Because all of you are talking about me, and everybody knows something that has to do with me, and I don't know anything," she said.

"I don't know more than you," I said.

"But you knew before I did," she said. "I don't like

that Jake went to Trina's and, especially—why didn't he tell me about it?"

"Exactly!" I said. "You should be mad at him! Not sad. Don't be sad."

She shrugged. "I don't want to talk anymore," she said. "Just take this and leave me alone. Okay?"

She held out my phone, and I took it.

"Are you sure I should go?" I said. "I want to stay. I don't want to go. I could help you finish unpacking."

"I'm sure," she said.

So I had to go. Because we don't share a room anymore. Which I am NOT liking right now. I need to know whether Jo is okay.

Tuesday, February 1

I just finished my second day of my new school. And two different people invited me to come home with them tomorrow! That's the good news. But there's bad news, too. Here's what happened:

I got to my classroom at 7:30 this morning. Since that's when Ms. Chanda said to meet her. She was there already, standing near her desk with Charlie and a tall woman wearing a pretty, long-sleeved dress with high boots.

"This is Charlie's mom, Mrs. Larken," Ms. Chanda told me. "She was just dropping Charlie off."

"Nice to meet you," I said.

"Nice to meet YOU!" Mrs. Larken said, with a big smile. "It's so good to have a new student in the class right now—you've started at a wonderful time!"

That made me think, *No, actually, I've started at a TERRIBLE time!* But I didn't want to disagree with her. She was so nice! And enthusiastic! I just smiled back, and she kissed Charlie goodbye and left.

Ms. Chanda explained a plan to me then.

"I've asked Charlie if he'd mind helping you get caught up," she said. "He has a knack for explaining difficult subjects. I'm here if you need me, but I'd like you to count on Charlie, too. Sound okay?"

"Sure," I said. Charlie reminded me of his mom, then, smiling at me. Except his face was a little pink. Probably because of Ms. Chanda's compliments.

"Perfect," Ms. Chanda said. "Was there anything in your homework that you had particular trouble with?"

"Rates of change," I said.

"I can help with rates of change!" Charlie said, enthusiastically.

Charlie and I sat together then and worked on rates of change problems. He really was good at explaining. I actually started to think I might understand.

But then we got distracted. Because Mary Majors RAN into the room and threw her arms into the air and shouted, "I'm early!" She was just a tiny bit out of breath.

"Good for you, Mary Majors," Ms. Chanda said. "Let's make this a new beginning."

"No problem, Ms. Chanda!" Mary Majors said. "I sprinted all eight blocks. I bet I'm faster than my oldest sister. And she won state in the 100, in track."

"With a little planning," Ms. Chanda said, "you wouldn't even have to sprint."

"My sister ran track, too," I told Mary Majors. "But she definitely did not win state."

Lots of kids started arriving then, and a group of girls surrounded Mary Majors. One of them said to her, "Are we still coming over tomorrow?" And another said, "We are, right?" Mary Majors said, "Yes, yes, yes!" as Ms. Chanda told everyone to start taking their seats. And they wandered off.

I felt a little bad, sitting there, in that moment. Because Mary Majors hadn't said a single word to me. I'd hoped she'd be super nice again, like she was yesterday. Plus I didn't love hearing her talk to those girls about getting together after school. I didn't expect them to include me—I couldn't even remember the other girls' names! But still. At my old school, I would've had friends to go home with. And here I had nobody.

Charlie must've seen my sadness. He got very serious. "DON'T let them upset you," he said. Then he said quickly, "You could come home with me tomorrow. If you want. I live close by. We could work on homework."

"Thanks!" I told him. It was such a nice thing to do! "I'll ask my mom—I'm sure she'll say yes. I live close, too!"

He gave me a happy smile. Ms. Chanda told us all to take out our science notebooks. And I decided to forget about Mary Majors.

But a few minutes later, as Ms. Chanda started talking about rocks and soil, a note landed on my desk.

Come over tomorrow after school!
Josie and Bella are. We'll hide in my sister's closet and spy on her and her friends. Not the track sister. The weight-lifter, basketball sister. You have to come!
M&M

After I read that note I had these thoughts: She invited me!! She still likes me!!

And: They're going to spy! I could bring my spy notebook!

And: How huge is the weight-lifter, basketball sister?!

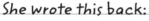

Finally I remembered the conversation I'd JUST had. And I passed Mary Majors a note saying, "Sorry! I'm going to Charlie's."

She wrote this back:

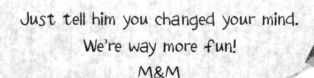

> Just tell him you changed your mind.
> We're way more fun!
> M&M

I sent back a note saying, "I can't. Too mean."

And she wrote this back:

> **Fine.** Choose Rover over us. Woof woof!
> Just Kidding.
> M&M

I don't like that note! I don't even understand it.
Why is she calling Charlie "Rover"? And barking
like a dog? Charlie doesn't look anything like a dog.

Besides, I like dogs.

> What kind
> of a name is
> Mary Majors?

At least she said just kidding.
Maybe it's an inside joke
they have?

I hope she invites me over again.

Huge news!

Mom just told me that we're hiring Eye-Della Stone, the Stranger Nurse they interviewed yesterday. She's moving in Friday, the day after Granny comes back!

I know we need a Stranger Nurse, and I'm glad Granny will have help. But I'm worried that Mom didn't do enough research!

She told me she'd called Eye-Della's references, and they had excellent things to say.

"Did you ask about Eye-Della's personal habits?" I said. Because I had very specifically reminded her to do that.

"A little," she said. Which was not an encouraging answer!

So I asked Mom about as many of Eye-Della's personal habits as I could think of. And it turns out Mom did NOT find out the answers to these very important questions:

1) Does Eye-Della Stone ALWAYS close the door when she uses the bathroom?

2) Does Eye-Della Stone KNOCK before opening closed bathroom doors? And bedroom doors, too?

3) How often does Eye-Della Stone shower?

4) How often does Eye-Della Stone get gassy?

5) Does Eye-Della Stone enjoy cooking stinky foods? Like boiled liver? Or eating disgusting foods, like TONGUE?

6) When Eye-Della Stone eats fish at home, does she leave the head on? Does she eat its EYES?

7) Does Eye-Della Stone always remember to flush?

8) Does Eye-Della clean her ears with her fingers and then look at her own earwax?

I can tell Mom is not planning to call Eye-Della Stone's references back to ask these questions. But this woman is going to live with us! We need to know!

Eat my EYES? What is WRONG with people?

# Right After Dinner

Lula and Violet just sent me bad texts! Here's what they say:

**Lula:** did you have a good day today, celie♥?

**Me:** it was ok. not as good as with both of you.

**Violet:** you need friends there, too! how's mary sergeants?

**Lula:** she means mary minors!

**Me:** haha, both of you. mary majors invited me over to her house tomorrow with other girls, which was nice. i can't go tho because i'm going to someone else's

**Violet:** who?

**Me:** charlie—in our class and also neighbor.

**Lula:** is charlie a boy????

**Me:** yes but just a friend!!! NOT a boyfriend,
i swear

**Violet:** can we talk about jo's boyfriend? he
went BACK to trina's today! and he brought
a COCONUT!

**Me:** that's TERRIBLE!

**Lula:** a coconut?

**Violet:** jo ate coconut on first date with jake.
and later when they had big fight, jake brought
coconut so she forgave him

**Lula:** how did i miss all that?

**Me:** he shouldn't bring coconuts to anyone but jo!

**Lula:** so he combines coconuts and dating?
is he dating trina?

**Violet:** he says he's not. but when I tell him to STOP GOING OVER THERE, he says i don't know what i'm talking about and should mind my own business. he's keeping his door closed all the time now, too. definitely keeping a secret.

**Me:** i have to tell jo, but I don't want to tell jo. she'll be sad!

**Lula:** what if you were going out with jake— or charlie!—and they started going out with trina, wouldn't you want to know?

**Me:** I AM NOT GOING OUT WITH CHARLIE!

**Lula:** jk, jk, don't worry

**Me:** have to go decide about jo now

**Lula:** tell her!

**Violet:** then tell us!

# After Being a Coward

I went to find Jo. She was smiling so big when I walked in her room! It was the first time I'd seen her smile at all since yesterday's bad Jake messages.

Now she sat so happy in her bed, with her phone beside her.

"Jake just texted," she said. "He's coming to visit! Two Sundays from now—the day before Valentine's Day. I'm so excited—isn't it exciting?"

I SHOULD'VE said, "Not exactly. Because he's already visited Trina, with a coconut."

But I wanted her to stay happy. So instead, I just said, "Mmn."

She SPRANG out of bed and said, "We need to finish setting up for Granny, right? Let's go!"

And we went.

Mom and Dad had already set up the furniture in Granny's room. The same arrangement as in our old apartment. Nice and familiar. Mom and I had put away all of Granny's clothes, too. And made her bed. But there were still important, missing steps.

First, Jo and I had to find Granny's white tablecloth with pretty blue flowers. We emptied A LOT of boxes in the living room before Jo found it, in a plastic bag, in the middle of a box full of yearbooks.

I told Dad he had to iron it. Because it had gotten very crinkly in that box.

He sang a weird old-timey song while he ironed.

...Let me call you sweetheart ...I'm in love with you.

Then Jo and I draped the tablecloth very neatly over Granny's desk. Like this:

We got Dad to hang Granny's painting of a crushed coffee cup, too. In the spot where it'd hung in her old room.

And, in a box labeled "Pics," we found the watercolor I'd painted of Granny when she was younger. She likes to keep it on her nightstand, so we set it there for her.

After that, Jo and I stood in Granny's doorway and

looked around. The room didn't look a hundred percent like her old one. This one's a little narrower, and the closet door is on the wrong side of her desk. But still. It's as close as we could get. So I said, "Perfect."

We had to go back to the living room then and put lots of things away. So Granny wouldn't get overwhelmed by boxes or mess. Or trip on anything.

Jo started singing "It's a Hard-Knock Life," from _Annie,_ as we cleaned up. I joined right in.

We used to sing _Annie_ songs together all the time, when we were little. We haven't done that in a very long time.

Maybe I should've talked to Jo about Jake instead of singing with her about cotton blankets instead of wool. But I really did not want to.

Today Jo and I went to school without a grownup for the first time in our whole lives! Mom and Dad let us walk together, since it's only four blocks.

"This is great, right?" I said to Jo, as we walked along.

She nodded and said, "Now they just have to let me ride the subway by myself. Practically every sixth grader I've ever met gets to do that."

Then she said, "It'd be so much easier to see Jake, if I could take the subway alone."

And THEN we passed the yummy-smelling bakery about a block from us. And she said, "This place looks so good. Jake and I should definitely come here when he visits, don't you think?"

I could've just said, "Sure." A big part of me wanted to just say, "Sure." Since I didn't want to ruin our nice walk.

74

But a bigger part of me didn't want to lie to Jo. And it felt like a big lie to let her keep thinking nice things about Jake. So I went ahead and said, "I have bad news about Jake."

"What are you talking about?" she said.

"Jake went to Trina's again yesterday," I told her. "He brought her a coconut. Violet texted me about it."

"Why would he go there again—and with a COCONUT? That makes no sense."

Before I could even say, "I know," she kept going.

"I ASKED him what he did yesterday after track," she said. "He didn't say ANYTHING AT ALL about Trina. What is he doing?"

"I don't kn—" I started to say. Again, she just kept going.

"Are you SURE he brought a coconut? I think maybe you misunderstood."

"I READ it," I said. "What other word looks like coconut?"

She didn't say anything then.

I started thinking about what Lula had said—about how I would feel if I was dating somebody who went to another girl's house and lied to me about it and brought her presents (even weird presents) that meant something between the two of us. I wouldn't like it AT ALL. I wasn't liking Jake at all—he wasn't treating Jo right.

So I said to Jo, "I think you should break up with him. I think Lula thinks that, too."

Jo stopped on the sidewalk outside of school then and said, "Wait—WHAT? What does Lula have to do with this? Did you have long talks with HER about me and Jake? AGAIN?"

She sounded so mad, but I hadn't done anything wrong! Of course Lula knew.

"She was on the texts," I told Jo. "The ones Violet sent. There were no long talks."

"You have to STOP gossiping about MY BUSINESS with the WHOLE WORLD!" Jo cried. "You and Lula and Violet don't know anything about anything!" She paused, red-faced and big-eyed, and pointed at me and said, "Nobody even LIKES you!"

Then she rushed away from me, toward school.

That was MEAN, I thought.

People like me, I thought.

Then I shouted at Jo, "I SHOULD'VE WALKED HERE WITH MOM OR DAD!"

She ignored me, yanked open the door of the school, and stomped inside.

I tried to think of people who like me, other than Lula and Violet. And Mom and Dad and Granny, who have to like me.

I was feeling pretty unliked when someone behind me said, "Wow, New Girl. What HAPPENED?"

I turned, and there was Mary Majors, looking concerned. And interested.

"Hey," I said.

I wanted to ask her, "Does anyone at this new school like me?" But that was too weird.

Instead I said, "You're early."

She shrugged. "My mom says if I get another detention she'll take the door off my bathroom. She doesn't care that I share it with my sisters, and that everyone could watch all of us pee. She says she'll do it anyway."

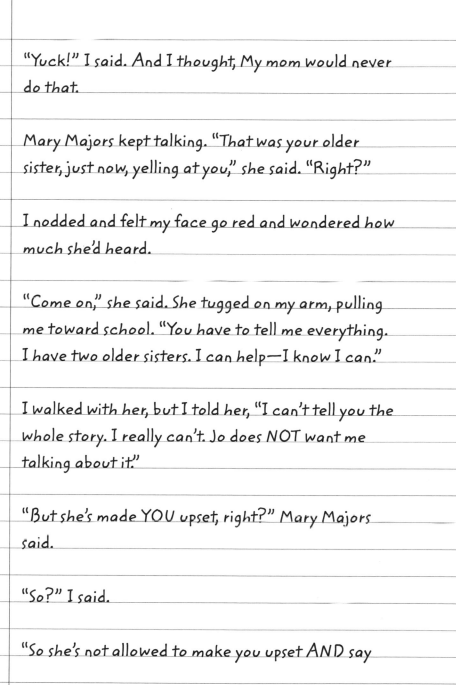

"Yuck!" I said. And I thought, My mom would never do that.

Mary Majors kept talking. "That was your older sister, just now, yelling at you," she said. "Right?"

I nodded and felt my face go red and wondered how much she'd heard.

"Come on," she said. She tugged on my arm, pulling me toward school. "You have to tell me everything. I have two older sisters. I can help—I know I can."

I walked with her, but I told her, "I can't tell you the whole story. I really can't. Jo does NOT want me talking about it."

"But she's made YOU upset, right?" Mary Majors said.

"So?" I said.

"So she's not allowed to make you upset AND say

you can't get help from other people, by talking
through what happened. That's not fair. My sisters
used to do that all the time. I don't listen anymore."

She's right—it's NOT fair, I thought.

"Plus I'm really good at keeping secrets, I swear,"
Mary Majors said. She raised her hand like she was
taking an oath and looked very serious. Then she
held the door to the school open for me. We saw
other kids then, in the foyer and lobby. She stepped
close to me, and whispered, "Don't say anything
now." Reminding me that they'd be able to hear.
Which was thoughtful of her.

Then she whispered, "I have the perfect secret
spot." And she hurried off down the hall.

I followed her. And I tried to decide what I could
tell her.

Finally I realized this: Mary Majors didn't know Jake
at all. So she couldn't possibly say the wrong thing

to him. The way Violet or Lula might (according
to Jo). So maybe I could say what I wanted to
Mary Majors. Especially if she was good at keeping
secrets. Plus I knew I'd be distracted all day long
if I didn't talk this through with somebody. And I
needed to be able to focus! I was already having
enough trouble understanding things like rates of
change and annotations!

At least Mary Majors was someone to talk to.

She pulled me into a girls' bathroom then.

"This spot is not secret," I told her.

"Hold on," she said. She checked all the stalls and
said, "Empty. Perfect."

Then she took a marker and paper out of her
backpack and wrote a note like this:

```
┌─────────────────────────────────────┐
│  HEALTH VIOLATIONS IN HERE.         │
│  PROPER AUTHORITIES CALLED.         │
│  USE OTHER BATHROOM.                │
└─────────────────────────────────────┘
```

"What a great sign!" I said.

"My oldest sister taught me," she said. "Hold on—I have to tape this."

She took tape out of her backpack, stuck her head out the door and looked up and down the hallway, then quickly taped up the sign.

After she came back in, she leaned against the door and said, "Tell me everything."

I had to tell her everything then. She'd gone to so much trouble!

She nodded as I talked. "Boyfriend problems," she said. "It's almost always boyfriend problems. My sisters always think I'm too young to help, but I'm not. I can fix this—I know it."

I was about to ask how, when someone started banging on the bathroom door.

Mary Majors opened the door, and we saw a man in a janitor's suit.

"What is this sign about?" he said.

"Hi, Stu!" Mary Majors cried. "Some kids must be playing a trick. Right, Celie?"

"Right!" I said. Because we were kids, and we were playing a trick.

"Don't worry," Mary Majors told Stu. "I'll take it down right now." She reached around the door to grab the sign, and Stu told us, "You two get on to class."

So we left, laughing, for class. After a minute, Mary Majors threw one arm around my shoulders and kept it there as we walked down the hall. "This way, if we bump into Jo, she'll definitely see that somebody likes you," Mary Majors told me.

I loved that she did that.

Later, in our classroom, when Ms. Chanda told us to get ready to go to art, Mary Majors stopped by my desk. "Saturday!" she said. "You have to come over Saturday. We'll make a plan!"

"I think that works!" I said. "I'll check."

"It has to!" she said.

She left to go back to her desk. I happened to look at Charlie then. He didn't look happy.

"What happened?" I said.

"It's just—Mary Majors," he said.

"Mary Majors what?" I said.

But he just said, "Later." Because Ms. Chanda was telling all of us to stop talking and start lining up.

I didn't forget that subject, though. I asked him about it after school, when I went to his house.

But I can't write about it now! My hand is tired! And my body is hungry! Too much happened today. I have to go get dinner. Will write more later.

## After Dinner

Now my body is happy! Because Mom made one of Granny's famous sour-cream coffee cakes, in celebration of Granny coming home tomorrow. It finished baking while we were eating dinner.

Mom thought she probably wouldn't have time to bake tomorrow. That's why she made it today.

Jo and I both said we should wait and eat it when Granny's with us.

"That was my first thought, too," Mom said. "But then I heard Granny's voice in my head, saying, 'This cake begs to be eaten fresh out of the oven. It's a crime to wait.' Can't you just hear her say that?"

I could definitely hear her say those exact words. But still. It's GRANNY'S famous cake! It seemed wrong to eat it without her.

"I don't know," I said.

"Let's have a little while it's warm, because she'd want us to," Dad said. "We'll save plenty to eat together."

So that's what we did. We each had one, small slice of cake fresh out of the oven, because Granny would want us to.

I am yummy deliciousness.

I've had my bath, too, and I'm comfy in bed. So I'm all ready to write about going to Charlie's this afternoon.

First of all, his family has its own townhouse. It's HUGE! And so pretty! I couldn't believe it when we walked in with his mom, after she'd picked us up from school. It was very light and white, with huge windows and flowy curtains. And that was only the first floor! There are THREE FLOORS!

Charlie's mom gave us popcorn at the kitchen table for snack. We started eating while she made herself tea at the stove. I was trying to think of something to say—I didn't want it to get too awkward and quiet. Then I remembered that I needed to ask Charlie something.

"What were you going to say about Mary Majors earlier?" I asked him. "Before art?"

Charlie didn't answer right away. His mom turned from the tea kettle and started watching him carefully. It felt funny—I worried I'd said something wrong.

Finally Charlie looked into his bowl of popcorn and said, "Did she tell you she doesn't like me?"

"No!" I said quickly. I didn't want them thinking for one second that I'd had bad conversations about Charlie with Mary Majors!

"Really?" Charlie said. He sounded so hopeful!

"Really," I told him. And I wasn't lying. She HADN'T said she didn't like him. She'd just called him dog names. Then said she was kidding.

"We used to be pretty good friends," he said. Very sadly.

That was all he would say about Mary Majors then. His mom kept watching him. She looked like she wanted to encourage him to keep talking. She must've decided not to, though. Because eventually she just said, "You two have fun. I'll be upstairs in my office if you need me." And she left with her mug of tea.

Charlie and I were down to the kernels in our popcorn bowls. I sat there and licked my fingers and wished his mom had told him to keep talking about Mary Majors. Because those two were the only possible friends I had so far! I needed to know whether they hated each other!

I decided to try again.

"Why would Mary Majors say she didn't like you?" I asked.

Charlie took our empty popcorn bowls to the sink and rinsed them and set them in the dishwasher. His mom hadn't even asked him to do that! I thought it was his way of ignoring my question. But I guess he was actually deciding to tell me the whole story. Because that's what he finally did. After he'd finished with the dishes and sat back down beside me.

"She found this break in the fence around the playground at school," he said. "A couple of weeks ago, behind some bushes. She started sneaking out onto the sidewalk during recess."

"Oh," I said, picturing that in my head. It was easy

to imagine Mary Majors sneaking off of school property, and not being worried one bit.

"She dared other kids to go out there, too," Charlie said. "Not me. She probably knew I wouldn't. But definitely Bella and Josie and Benjamin. I heard her say she'd steal her sister's stopwatch, so they could time who stayed out the longest. And she wanted to have a contest to see who'd go the farthest."

I could imagine that, too. I could hear her in my head saying, "Come on, New Girl. It'll be so fun!"

"I didn't like it," Charlie said. "I thought someone could get kidnapped. Or a stranger could sneak through that break in the fence someday with a knife, while the kindergartners were on the playground."

"Poor kindergartners!" I said.

"I know," Charlie said. "So I told a teacher about

the fence. And it got fixed. I did NOT rat on Mary Majors. I never said she left. But she knows I'm the reason the fence got fixed. And she keeps calling me Teacher's Pet. And Spot. And Whiskers."

And Rover, I thought.

"I think you did the right thing," I told him.

"Thanks," he said. But he still sounded sad.

"I'll only ever call you Charlie," I told him. "Or Mr. Larken, if you want. Or Sir Charles Larken."

That made him laugh. So I called him things like Professor Larken for the rest of the afternoon. And we did lots of homework. Plus he put his number in my phone, so I can call him whenever I need homework help. That was all very useful.

It was a good afternoon. Except, I feel confused— not about homework, but about Mary Majors. Because I know she shouldn't call Charlie those names. Or lie to grownups, or sneak off school property, or put the lives of kindergartners in danger.

But still. She's been so nice to me. Saving seats for me at lunch and inviting me over more than once and helping me with my fight with Jo.

I only have two friends at this school. I don't want to give either one of them up.

I want to sleep.

I just had a fight with Jo.

She came into my room while I was finishing getting dressed for school. And she said, "I talked to Jake. He says Violet doesn't know what she's talking about, and I should trust him, not his baby sister."

"Violet is not a baby!" I said. "And she DOES know what she's talking about. She's a smart person."

"She's not with him all the time," Jo said. "And neither are you."

"Neither are YOU," I said.

"Just—don't talk to me about Jake ever again," she said. Then she stomped out of my room.

So this day has gotten off to a really good start.

Me, Going Back to Sleep

## Later, After School

It's hard to deal with both Mary Majors and Charlie! I TRIED today. When Mary Majors stopped by my desk again, while Charlie and I were both sitting there.

She asked what was up with Jo. So I told her about the fight. She said not to worry—she had a perfect plan for us, for when I came over on Saturday.

I couldn't really focus on that. Because I was

distracted by Charlie. Knowing he was sitting right there, hearing everything. I didn't want him to think I was abandoning him for someone who called him dog and cat names. Or going back on my promise to never call him those things.

Finally I tried to include him. I didn't know what to say, though. Because Charlie doesn't know anything about the whole Jo situation.

I ended up saying the only, stupid thing I could think of. Which was, "Charlie lives in this neighborhood. Did you know that, Mary Majors?"

She raised her eyebrows at me and said, "I've been to Charlie's house a million times." Then she just left.

So that part of my day didn't exactly go well, either.

## Nighttime

Now my day is officially TERRIBLE. But it should've gotten better! Because Granny is home!

Cousin Carla dropped her off after dinner, then didn't stay. Which was fine with me, since Cousin Carla tends to do very embarrassing things. Like talking about her period. But the REASON she didn't stay was RIDICULOUS. She had a POLE DANCING class. She's FORTY! Why is she learning how to dance around poles?

Anyway. We all kissed Granny, and she kissed us, and we said things like, "We're so happy you're finally here!" Then we gave her a tour of our whole apartment.

She seemed to like it. She said things like "Oh, this is very nice." And, "You found a very good place."

But then we got to HER room. That's when things turned bad.

"This one's for you," Dad said, leading her inside.

"For me?" she said. She laughed a little. "You're being silly."

"We set it all up for you," I told her.

The wrinkle between her eyebrows got deeper. Then she smiled at me and said, "You're a sweet girl."

"Thanks, Granny," I said.

She turned to Dad and said, "She's such a sweet girl."

"She is," he said. "And she was a big help, fixing up this room for you."

Granny's smile got a little smaller. "I have a room already, thank you," she said, looking only at Dad's face.

Mom spoke up then, from just behind me. "We moved from our old apartment, Granny, remember? We all live here now."

Granny nodded slowly. She was obviously doing some thinking.

Then she said to Mom, "I have a room, at 2304

South Lovelace. It's pale green, with twin beds and pink bedspreads."

She turned to Dad and said, "Mama chose the bedspreads. I don't like them—I told her I don't like them—but she won't buy me new ones."

My heart tumbled to the floor then. Because I could tell Granny was talking about her bedroom from when she was a girl. And I hated seeing her so confused.

Dad and Mom looked at each other, and we were all very quiet. For too long a time.

Finally Jo said, "We have sour-cream coffee cake—does anyone want some?"

It was EXACTLY the right thing to do. Granny clapped her hands together and said, "I love sour-cream coffee cake."

We all sat together at the kitchen table then, and Mom set out slices of cake. After Granny had tasted hers, she said, "This is delicious. But you know, the perfect time to eat this cake is fresh out of the oven."

"We knew you'd say that!" Jo told her. "So we ate some then."

"AND we saved lots for you," I said.

"How nice," Granny said. And we all finished eating.

Then Mom persuaded Granny to go look at her room again. "I just want to show you some things," Mom said.

Dad told me and Jo to go finish our homework and get ready for bed.

"Don't worry," he told us. "Mom and I will get Granny settled and happy. I promise."

So I finished my homework and put on my pajamas and tried not to worry. But on my way to the bathroom to brush my teeth, I heard Granny say, "It's dark out already. Mama will be worried."

I hated hearing that.

I listened carefully on my way back, too. I heard Mom reading to Granny. Which was better.

And, a little while later, Mom and Dad both came in my room, to tell me that Granny had fallen asleep.

"She'll improve as she gets used to the space," Mom said. "You'll see. We don't want you to worry."

"Exactly," Dad said. "Your job is NOT to worry. Your job is to sleep. Got it?"

I nodded, and they kissed me goodnight and went off to their room.

But still, I worried. I thought things like, What if Granny tries to leave our apartment and go back to South Lovelace? What if she makes it outside, then somehow makes it onto a bus that she thinks is going to South Lovelace, wherever that is? And then gets off in the middle of nowhere and has no idea how to get back? And we have no idea how to find her? Or what if she can't get on a bus because she leaves without money, and she tries to hitchhike instead? And ends up kidnapped by the driver of a big truck?

I couldn't let any of that happen. So I took my pillow and my blanket, and this journal and my flashlight, and I tiptoed to the foyer.

I'm sitting in front of the front door now. I'm staying here all night. That way, if Granny tries to get out, I'll know. And I can stop her.

## MIDDLE OF THE NIGHT

Jo's here! In the foyer, with her pillow and blanket. She had the same idea I did.

She might be stupid about boys, but she's still my perfect, brilliant sister.

Nobody's getting in or out of this place.

School was NOT GOOD today! This is how I looked, all day:

Because it is NOT EASY to sleep on the floor in our foyer.

Charlie actually asked, "Are you okay? Do you need me to take you to the nurse?" That's how bad it was.

This was the other bad thing about school: Ms. Chanda is in love with weekend homework! I have a quiz on rates of change AND medians and modes—which she just taught us today!—plus I have to write a story about being a Dutch settler in New York, plus I have to memorize 20 spelling words.

I MISS MY OLD SCHOOL!

At least I can call Charlie for help.

## Later

Eye-Della is here! Mom helped her get all set up in her room, and introduced her to everybody. Even though Jo and I met her already, on the day of her interview.

Then Mom said to Eye-Della and Granny, "Why don't you two get to know each other while I make dinner?" And they sat down together in the living room.

I had to spy! To make sure Eye-Della treats Granny right when she thinks no one else is around.

Here is my spy report:

## From the
# Top-Secret Spy Notebook of

Celie Valentine Altman

**Spies must be fit, because at any moment they might need to escape a dangerous situation or confront an enemy. How far and fast could you flee, if you were to need to disappear into the night?**

NOBODY in this family is disappearing into the night. Eye-Della is going to help with that.

**Do you have sufficient training to fight and vanquish your foe, should the need arise?**

Is Eye-Della my foe? Because I am definitely not allowed to fight Eye-Della. Or any other old lady. I'm not even supposed to hit or kick Jo.

Except, I would DEFINITELY hit and kick Eye-Della if she hurt Granny.

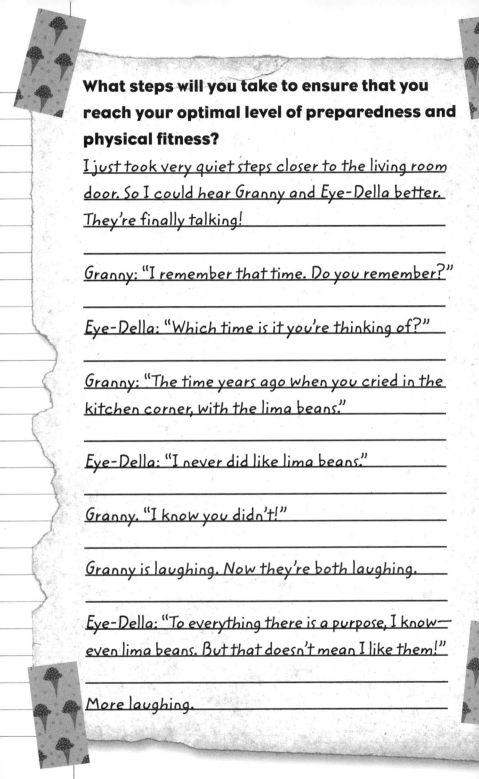

**What steps will you take to ensure that you reach your optimal level of preparedness and physical fitness?**

I just took very quiet steps closer to the living room door. So I could hear Granny and Eye-Della better. They're finally talking!

Granny: "I remember that time. Do you remember?"

Eye-Della: "Which time is it you're thinking of?"

Granny: "The time years ago when you cried in the kitchen corner, with the lima beans."

Eye-Della: "I never did like lima beans."

Granny. "I know you didn't!"

Granny is laughing. Now they're both laughing.

Eye-Della: "To everything there is a purpose, I know— even lima beans. But that doesn't mean I like them!"

More laughing.

I had to stop spying then, because Mom called me from the kitchen, to help her with the twice-baked potatoes.

I love twice-baked potatoes.

I'm also liking Eye-Della so far. Because:

1) She sits nicely with Granny, and she would notice if Granny got up to go to South Lovelace.

2) She talks nicely to Granny, too, even when Granny is not making sense. For example, Granny couldn't have seen Eye-Della cry in the kitchen corner with lima beans years ago. She didn't even know Eye-Della years ago. But Eye-Della didn't argue one bit with Granny.

Eye-Della

not gassy

3) As far as I can tell so far, Eye-Della is not unusually gassy.

I am in BIG trouble right now. I have never been in so much trouble. And it's mostly Mary Majors's fault. I don't think I'll ever forgive her.

I can't believe how much has happened just today—and it's only a little after three! At least I have plenty of time to write about it here. Since Mom and Dad say I can't leave my room until one of them comes to get me.

No TV. No computer, either. No phone of any kind. I don't even know what they've done with my beautiful cell phone.

Will I ever see you again?

Here's how all my problems started:

This morning Mom walked me over to Mary Majors's apartment. She kept pointing out what a beautiful day it was, and she was right. Even though it's still very cold out. The sky was very blue, with no clouds. Plus no wind. It definitely seemed like the kind of day when nothing could go wrong.

Mary Majors's apartment is nice, but messy! When she opened the door for us, we saw coats thrown over chairs and shoes kicked everywhere—

kneepads on the floor, too—and backpacks on the sofa and dirty dishes on the coffee table.

"Is your mom home?" Mom asked Mary Majors. "Or your dad?"

"They're showing apartments," Mary Majors said. "They're brokers. But my sisters are here. They're teenagers, and they stay with me alone all the time. So you don't have to worry."

Mom definitely still looked worried.

"May I speak with a sister, please?" she said, and I said, "Mom!" Because she was so obviously not trusting Mary Majors.

But Mary Majors just said, "Sure." Then she shouted, "LAYLA! COME TO THE DOOR! WE NEED YOU!"

We waited then. I tried not to look at all the mess. I wanted so badly to pick some of it up.

Finally we heard footsteps, and a very pretty teenager with a high, swinging ponytail hurried down the hall toward us. She smiled at my mom and said, "Everything okay?"

Mom looked so relieved.

"I'm just dropping Celie off," she said. "Should I call later, to see what time to pick her up?"

"Sure," Layla said.

"Parents always love Layla," Mary Majors whispered to me.

Then Mom kissed me and said, "Call me if you need me."

She went outside, and Layla went back down the hall, and Mary Majors and I were alone in the mess.

"Text your friend," Mary Majors told me. "The one who's the sister of your sister's boyfriend."

"Violet?" I said. "Why?"

"Make sure she's going to be home today," Mary Majors said. "We're going to go see her. And figure out what's up with her brother."

"We ARE?" I said.

"If she's home," Mary Majors said. "My sister can take us. I already asked her."

Part of me loved that plan. I really, really wanted to see Violet. My parents kept saying they'd pick a time for a visit, but they never had. And they were so busy with everything! At this rate I might never see her again! Maybe Lula could even come, too!! It'd be weird seeing them with Mary Majors, but at least I'd get to see them. I missed them both so much.

Part of me hesitated, though. What if Mary Majors started asking questions about Jo and Jake while we were there, and later Jo found out about it?

It was definitely possible. Then Jo would know that
I'd talked about her problems with ANOTHER
friend, and she'd want to kill me.

Except, Jo already wanted to kill me. Whether or
not we went to Violet's. Plus, I figured, maybe Mary
Majors could help figure Jo's problems out. She was
sometimes a big help. Maybe she'd have creative
ideas. Like that bathroom sign.

And also, I needed to see my best friends!

So I texted Violet, who WAS home. She texted back
things like, "Yay, yay, yay!" And, "I can't wait to
meet Mary Minors!" And, "Of course I'll see if Lula
can come!"

These texts made me so happy.

But then I told Mary Majors, "I just have to call my
mom and let her know we're going."

Right away, Mary Majors said, "Don't do that!"

"Why not?" I said.

"BECAUSE," Mary Majors said. Sounding like she shouldn't even have to explain. "She might say no, since it's not exactly close by. Then we won't be able to find out whether your sister's boyfriend is lying to her. But if you DON'T call, then your mom can't say no."

I hesitated. Mom DEFINITELY thought I was staying at Mary Majors's. She would NOT want me going an hour away. I knew that.

But still—I wanted to see Violet! And maybe Lula! And Mary Majors had a point: If I called Mom for permission, she probably would say, "You can do that another day." But that other day might never come!

Plus Jo needed me! Jake was being bad!

Then I thought about it this way: What if Mary Majors's sister took us out for lunch? Or took us to the bakery for a snack? Would Mom care about that? No, she would not. This wasn't so different. It was still just the sister taking us somewhere.

That thinking helped me a lot with my decision.

"Let's do it," I told Mary Majors.

"Perfect!" she said, bouncing up and down on her toes. Then she turned and shouted, "SHAYNA!! LET'S GO!!"

Shayna? I thought. What happened to Layla?

Then a door slammed, and a different teenager walked toward us. A taller, wider, and grumpier teenager than Layla.

I figured it was the weight-litter, basketball sister.

She didn't even say hi to me. She just said, "I can't believe I'm doing this." Then she pointed at Mary Majors and said, "I don't ever want to hear about that picture again."

"I promise," Mary Majors said. Very seriously.

"Where exactly are we going?" Shayna said.

I told her Violet's address, and she looked up directions.

While she did, Mary Majors whispered to me, "I have a picture of her drinking beer from our fridge, with her friends."

"Oh," I said. And I thought, BEER!!! That's BAD!!!

Then Shayna said, "This is going to take FOREVER. Let's go."

She walked about a half a block ahead of us the whole way to the subway. She didn't even turn back to make sure we weren't getting hit by cars when we crossed streets. After she swiped a MetroCard to get us all into the train station, she moved pretty far from us on the platform. And sat many seats away from us on both of the trains we took. And barely talked to us at all.

Mary Majors and I had fun on the walk and on the first train, at least for a while. She asked me questions like, "Would you rather be completely bald—and not be allowed to wear a wig or a hat—or completely deaf?" And, "Would you rather give up baths and showers for the rest of your life, or give up desserts?"

That game was fun until she said, "Would you rather kiss Charlie, or lick a gorilla's foot?" And I had to say, "I don't like it when you're mean to Charlie." Because I don't.

We were quiet after that. And Shayna was right—it did take a really long time to get there.

But at least Violet's apartment is close to the subway. And I knew exactly how to get there, once we came out of the stop. So I led the way.

I wanted to stop at so many places! The bagel store owned by a very nice family, and Mom's favorite bookstore, and the jewelry store where Lula got her ears pierced. I was so close to my

old building, too! It would only have been a
few blocks out of the way—I could've seen the
outside, at least!

But I knew none of those spots meant anything to
Mary Majors or Shayna. Plus Shayna obviously didn't
want to take even one step more than she had to.
Also, I wasn't a hundred percent sure I wanted to go
to my building, since it's not actually mine anymore.
I didn't want to look up at our windows and see
somebody else moving around in that apartment.
Maybe even in my old room.

So I walked us straight to Violet's pretty brownstone,
in the middle of a block lined with other homes like
it. We got there fast, and I said, "This is it."

What happened next is very hard to believe. But
I can't write it yet, because there's a lot to say
and I have to pee. And that situation is only going
to get worse. Plus I need a slice of sour-cream
coffee cake.

A LITTLE LATER

Dad gave me a bathroom break. But not a slice of sour-cream coffee cake. Just a handful of celery sticks. Then he sent me back to my room.

Celery sticks are very sad.

I make everything worse.

Anyway. Back to my crazy, horrible day:

After I'd led us right to Violet's brownstone, Mary Majors told Shayna, "I TOLD you she'd know where to go." Which made me feel good.

But then Shayna said to Mary Majors, "I am NOT sticking around. That's not part of the deal. You have a way to get home, right?" Which did NOT make me feel good!

"What did you just say?" I asked Shayna. But she and Mary Majors both ignored me. And Mary

Majors told Shayna, "We'll be fine." And Beer-Drinking Shayna turned and WALKED AWAY!
Back the way we'd come, just leaving us there! We hadn't even climbed the steps to Violet's door and rung her bell! It could've been empty in there for all she knew!

"Where is she going?!" I asked Mary Majors. "We're supposed to have one of your sisters with us! That's why I didn't call my parents! How are we supposed to get home?! WHY DID YOU TELL HER WE'D BE FINE?"

"Because we will be fine," Mary Majors said. "Violet's mom'll probably take us home." Then she started climbing up the steps to Violet's door.

"Violet's mom?!" I said, following her. "We haven't even asked her! And she's always busy! Get your sister back here!"

I turned to look for Shayna, thinking I'd run after her myself. But I couldn't see her anymore—she must've turned the corner.

"Don't worry so much," Mary Majors said. Then she went ahead and rang the bell. Of MY friend's home! Which made me annoyed. I know anyone can ring a bell. But she shouldn't have been doing that! She should've been controlling her terrible sister!

Then the door opened and Violet was hugging me and jumping up and down.

"I've missed you!" she said. "Lula is so jealous! But her dad's family is in town."

I hated being so close and not seeing Lula. But I was still happy to see Violet.

I introduced Mary Majors, and Violet's mom waved at us as she walked by, talking on the phone. Then Violet said, "What do you want to do?"

I hesitated for a second. What DID I want to do? Did I want to figure out how we were getting home, before we did anything else? Did I really want to investigate Jake with Mary Majors there? When I knew Jo would hate it? I felt all mixed up.

While I was thinking, Mary Majors said to Violet, "Can we talk in your room?"

"Sure," Violet said. It seemed like a fine idea to me, too. So we all went upstairs.

On the second floor we could hear the shower running in the bathroom on our left.

"Is that Jake in there?" Mary Majors asked. Sounding VERY interested.

"Yes," Violet said slowly. I could tell she was wondering, Why do you care if my brother's in the shower? I wondered what Mary Majors was thinking, too. I didn't have a good feeling about it.

And I was right about that. Because Mary Majors said, "This timing is PERFECT! Which one is his room?"

"Why?" Violet said. She gave me a look that said, "What's going on?" I told Mary Majors, "Let's just go to VIOLET'S room."

But Mary Majors had already found Jake's room on her own. Because the door to the room across from the bathroom was open. And the word "JAKE" was painted in huge letters on a wall.

Mary Majors hurried right in.

"What are you DOING?" Violet said.

"Celie needs to know whether Jake is cheating on Jo," Mary Majors said. "To protect her sister. So we have to spy."

"This was not my idea!" I told Violet, who was looking very outraged. The way I'd look if a stranger came into my apartment and demanded to search my sister's room.

"You don't have permission to be in here," Violet told Mary Majors.

Mary Majors ignored her, walked over to Jake's desk, looked through some papers, then lifted one high and said, "Ha! Got it!"

"Got what?" I said. I couldn't help being curious.

"Whatever it is, put it back," Violet said.

"This says, 'Love Song,'" Mary Majors said. "He's writing a love song! But who is he writing it TO?"

Who IS he writing it to? I thought. It better not be Trina.

Then the bathroom door opened! And Jake was standing there IN A TOWEL!

"Aaaggh!" I said. And half-hid my eyes with my hand. Because I can't see Jake when he's just in a towel!

He said, "Aagh!" too, and took two steps backwards. Then he stopped and said to Mary Majors, "Who ARE you?" And to all of us he said, "What are you DOING? GET OUT OF MY ROOM!"

"I said the same thing!" Violet told him. "I really did!"

"She did," I said. "Also, this wasn't my idea."

But Mary Majors said, "We are NOT LEAVING until we know who you are writing this song to." And she held that sheet of paper up high.

"Give me that!" Jake said. He starting reaching and trying to grab it. But he couldn't do a very good job. Because he had to hang on tight to his towel.

Mary Majors darted away from him. Then she actually climbed onto his bed and stood on her tiptoes and held the paper as high as she possibly could.

I could not believe what I was seeing. But it definitely worked. Jake couldn't jump and grab in a towel. He stood with one hand holding the towel and one hand curled in a fist instead. He obviously wanted to PUNCH Mary Majors!

She paid no attention to that. Instead she started READING THE PAPER. Right in front of him!

"You can't read that!" Violet said. "It's private!"

I almost said, "She's right." Because Mary Majors should NOT have barged into Jake's room, taken his love writing, and read it while he was telling her not to! But still—if Jake was writing a love song to Trina, he was acting badly, too! And I needed to know if he was doing that to my sister. So I didn't say a word to Mary Majors.

She read for a minute more. Then she said, "What does this mean?" And she read out loud, "'And that time you forgave me/For telling your granny's secret.'"

She looked at Jake, actually expecting him to explain his private, stolen love song to her! When she did, she forgot to hold the paper high, and he reached out and YANKED it out of her hand.

"NOW GET OUT!" he shouted.

While he was yanking and shouting, something clicked in my head.

"You told JO'S granny's secret!" I said. "That song is for Jo!" Because he got in big trouble with me and Jo a while ago, when he told his mom that Granny accidentally started a fire in our kitchen. No one was supposed to know that.

"Of course it's for Jo," he said, looking at me like I was an idiot. "Who else would it be for?"

"Trina," I said.

"I would NEVER write a love song for TRINA," Jake said. He sounded disgusted.

"Then why do you keep going to her apartment?" I said.

"And why'd you bring a coconut?" Violet said. (I was so happy to hear her say that! Because she could definitely have sided entirely against me, after everything Mary Majors had done.)

Jake was glaring at Violet now. "I TOLD you to stop telling her where I was going!" He pointed an angry finger at me. "Now look what's happened!"

"This isn't my fault!" Violet said.

"It really isn't," I said. I was ready to leave then. Violet and Jake almost never fought—I knew that. I hated seeing him so angry with her because of me.

But crazy Mary Majors said, "We are not going anywhere until we get the explanation Jo deserves." Even though she barely knew Jo!

Then she sat down in the middle of Jake's bed and folded her arms across her chest. Obviously prepared to wait.

"If I tell you," Jake said, "would you all GET OUT OF MY ROOM?"

"We definitely will," I said. "I promise."

He waited, looking at Mary Majors, right in the middle of his bed.

"I'll get her out, too," I said.

He sighed and looked up at the ceiling and started speaking fast. "I wasn't going to see TRINA," he said. "I was going to see her BROTHER. He's a musician. He has flyers up in coffee shops, saying he can help write songs. I recognized his picture. I wanted to do something nice for Jo for Valentine's Day. He told me to bring things that remind me of her. I brought the coconut."

He looked at me then and said very loudly, "THAT IS THE END OF THE STORY, OKAY? GET OUT OF MY ROOM NOW!"

I thought he might explode in a million pieces. I was ready to pull Mary Majors out if I had to. But she jumped off the bed by herself and ran out of the room. I hurried after her. Violet stayed with Jake, though. I heard him saying things like "NOT OKAY"

and "HOW WOULD YOU LIKE IT!" and "YOU'D
BETTER HIDE YOUR THINGS FROM MY FRIENDS!"

Violet stayed in there for a while. When she finally
came out, she said to me, "He's really mad. I don't
want to kick you out, but . . ." She paused and shook
her head. Then she gave me a look that said, "Why
would you bring that crazy girl to my house? And
get me in trouble with my brother? How could you
DO that to me? I thought you were my friend!"

I felt very mixed up and terrible then. Everything
had gone so wrong! I'd wanted to help Jo, but I'd
never, ever planned to break into Jake's room and go
through his papers and demand explanations from
him while he was practically naked! And I'd really
wanted a nice visit with Violet. I missed her! I might
not get to see her again for months! But I'd barely
even talked to her! Plus I'd gotten Jake furious with
her. All because Mary Majors was a LUNATIC!

I didn't know how to tell Violet all of that. The only
thing I could think to say was, "I'm so sorry."

"We could go now, if it'd be better for you," Mary Majors told Violet. Making herself sound thoughtful and generous, now that she'd ruined everything.

I wanted Violet to say, "I need to talk this through with Celie first." Or, "You can't go—I never get to see Celie—the visit can't end in such a bad way!"

But instead she nodded and said, "It'd probably be better if you left."

I tried to shoot laser beams out of my eyes at Mary Majors then. Like this:

But it didn't work. Mary Majors stayed in one piece. And we all started walking downstairs together.

Then, suddenly, I remembered a problem. And I asked Violet, "Can I say goodbye to your mom?" Because I needed her to take us home!

"Sure," Violet said. Together we found her mom, who had two other women with her now. They were sitting around the dining room table with papers set out in front of them. Obviously having a meeting.

"That was a fast visit," Violet's mom said, when Violet told her I was leaving. "Is everything okay? I thought I heard some commotion up there."

"We're fine," Violet told her. "It's just time for Celie to go."

"Oh—are your parents here to pick you up?" Violet's mom asked. "I'll come say a quick hi. I was sorry not to see them when they dropped you off."

133

"They didn't bring us," I told her. Very honestly. "Mary Majors's older sister did."

"How nice to have a sibling old enough to take you places," Violet's mom said. "We're counting down the days."

Then, before I could say anything else, one of the other women handed Violet's mom a sheet of paper and said, "What do you think of the first two paragraphs, Betsy?" And Violet's mom said to Violet, "You'll see them out, right?" She gave me a quick hug and said, "So good to see you, Celie." Then she started reading that paper. And I didn't say anything like, "Would you please stop reading that paper and leave these women here and travel more than an hour to take me home and more than an hour back?" Because she obviously could not do that.

Instead I followed Violet, who led me and Mary Majors to her front door and opened it for us. I thought she might say, "Where is that older sister?" Since there was not a single person there to pick us up. But she didn't.

Maybe she was still thinking through what had happened upstairs, and she didn't even notice. Or maybe she just assumed the older sister was waiting somewhere nearby. Like a normal, responsible person. I don't know.

All I know is, the only thing Violet said to me was, "Bye." Then she locked the door behind us.

So I stood at the top of her stoop. Feeling pushed out by one of my very best friends, with the door locked forever behind me.

I don't want to write any more right now.

## A Little Later

Granny came to visit me! She brought me a big slice of sour-cream coffee cake because she heard me ask Mom and Dad for one earlier. At first I thought maybe she didn't realize that I was in trouble. But before she left, she raised a finger to her lips then pointed at the cake and whispered, "Our little secret."

It's the best secret in the world.

I hope this means she doesn't think I'm bad. I HATE the idea of Granny thinking I'm bad.

# After A Little Digesting

It's NOT going to be easy to see Mary Majors at school on Monday. For one thing, after Violet locked us out, we had a big fight on the sidewalk.

"You ruined everything!" I told her.

"I did not!" she told me. She actually looked really surprised. "I SAVED everything. I found out what Jake was doing! And it's good for Jo! She's going to be so happy."

It was true that she'd been good for Jo. But in such a bad way!

"I wish you'd done it differently," I told her.

She looked like she had no idea what I was talking about. Which was annoying!

"We don't even have a way home now!" I told her. "HOW ARE WE GETTING HOME?"

She bit her lip instead of answering, and I wanted to cry. I didn't have money for a taxi, so I couldn't even try to figure out how to take one without a grownup. And I knew it was a five-hour walk. And I didn't know the way. And I needed my parents, and I couldn't stand how upset and disappointed in me they were going to be when I reached them.

"Can you call your parents? Or Layla?" I asked Mary Majors. She shook her head and said, "They're all working."

"My parents will be SO MAD that I went this far away without asking permission," I said. "I should've called my mom before we left!"

"We could take the subway," Mary Majors said.

"I'm not allowed to take the subway by myself!" I said. "I'm ten! Jo isn't even allowed to take the subway by herself!"

"But nobody will ever know," she said. She sounded a little excited—like it might be even better to secretly ride the subway alone. I did not agree with that! But I couldn't figure out what to do.

"You know how to get to the subway station, right?" she asked.

"Yes," I said. "But I've never been on a subway without a grownup! What if there's a crazy man on the train? Talking to himself and lying across a bunch of seats and not wearing shoes? That happens."

"You were just on the subway with Shayna," Mary Majors said. "She's not a grownup. She didn't sit with us—she barely even looked at us! Plus we can check for crazy people before we get on. If we see something scary, we'll go to the next car."

"I don't know," I said. I imagined myself on a subway platform, running away from a crazy person, trying to get into the next car before the doors closed, and then getting stuck in the doors.

Mary Majors kept talking. "We only have to take

two trains," she said. "The F and the A. I paid attention. I have a little money, too. Enough for a MetroCard for both of us. It'll be great!"

I definitely did not think it would be great. But she was making it seem okay.

"Besides," she said, "the only other option is to call your parents, and it would take them at least an hour to get here. What are we going to do for an hour? They wouldn't want us just standing here on the street. It's cold!"

I didn't say anything.

"It's going to be JUST THE SAME as it was with Shayna!" Mary Majors said. "Except better, because she won't ruin it with her grumpiness."

I had to admit—Shayna hadn't helped us at all. Plus I didn't want to call my parents. And it was freezing out. And it was just getting later and later, and I wasn't getting anywhere!

"Fine," I said. "Let's go."

We walked back to the subway station, to get on the F train. I didn't like walking down the steps alone. I kept noticing things I'd never focused on before. Like the bits of ceiling hanging down, and the peeling paint, and the flickering of the yellow lights, and the shadows. I knew there were rats in the subway sometimes—what if one came out of the shadows?

I wanted to say, "Stop—this is a TERRIBLE idea." But Mary Majors had already fed her dollars into the MetroCard machine and was pressing buttons. Soon it spat out a card, and Mary Majors walked to the turnstiles and swiped the card twice very smoothly, and said, "Let's go!" So I went.

I wasn't even sure which stairs to take next. But we followed the big black sign that said "Manhattan & Queens." What if we end up in QUEENS? I thought. I don't know anything about Queens!

Then we heard the sound of a train roaring in, and Mary Majors said, "Hurry!" And I followed as she ran down more flights of stairs.

By the time we got to the bottom, we heard the conductor announce, "Stand clear of the closing doors, please." Mary Majors RACED into a car, without checking first for crazy people! I had to race after her. We couldn't get separated!

Before I could even say, "You didn't check!" Mary Majors scared me for ANOTHER reason. Because she said, "Wait, is this an F? It could be a G." But the doors were closing! The train was moving! It was the wrong time to figure out whether this was an F!

"How do we tell if it's an F?" I cried. Then Mary Majors turned to a COMPLETE STRANGER and said, "Is this an F?"

Fortunately, the stranger said, "Yes." And also, the stranger was a nice woman with a cute baby in a stroller. So we sat close to them. Then Mary Majors asked the woman, "Do you know how we get to the A?" I almost yelled, "YOU DON'T KNOW HOW TO GET TO THE A?!" Because she'd told me she'd paid attention!! We were going to end up in Queens!!

But the woman knew all about the A. She told us we needed to transfer at the Jay Street-MetroTech station, and she made sure we got off there. We waved goodbye from the platform as the doors to the F closed, and the nice woman and her baby rode away.

And then, DISASTER!!! Because as we were following signs for the A train, we kept hearing announcements like this: "Due to a blah-blah-blah-something, Manhattan-bound A trains are not stopping at Jay Street-MetroTech Please use alternate service."

"We need alternate service!" I told Mary Majors.

"I don't know any alternate service!" she told me.

We asked one woman, but she couldn't help, and there were scary men EVERYWHERE in that station—some of them with no teeth! We couldn't ask THEM! And the station was huge and dark and weirdly wet and crumbly, and I didn't want to just stand still, staring at a route map.

I started following exit signs, and Mary Majors followed me; and we finally got out of that terrible place.

"Where ARE we?" Mary Majors said, when we came out of the station.

"I have no idea!" I said.

"But you're from Brooklyn! We're still in Brooklyn!" she said.

"Brooklyn is HUGE!" I cried. Then I said, "I'm calling my mom."

I took out my phone and saw that I had five missed

calls from Jo and about fifteen texts—also from Jo.
Texts like this:

"mom and dad at movies, to celebrate finishing
move. asked me to come pick u up. answer ur
phone!"

and

"where r u?"

and

"looked up Mary Majors in school directory. no one
answering at her house. WHERE R U?"

and

"call me right now!"

and

"I AM FREAKING OUT!"

I wasn't paying enough attention to people around me as I read those texts. When I finished, I realized that Mary Majors was trying to hide behind me and whispering, "That guy's staring at me. I'm scared."

Many VERY LARGE boys were pushing each other and shouting bad words at a corner near us. And one of them was STARING in our direction.

AAAAAAGH! I thought. I hid my phone behind my back for second—I didn't want them to steal it! Except, I needed to use it!

"Come ON!" I said to Mary Majors, and I PULLED on her until I got her around the corner. She was weirdly frozen. And the block felt too deserted—I wanted more people! I tried and I tried and I tried to call Jo, but I got voicemail every time. I kept thinking, What's the MATTER with her?! SHE SHOULD BE PICKING UP!!!

"Who else can I call?" I asked Mary Majors.

She didn't answer. She was looking behind us, waiting. "They might follow us," she whispered. "One of them pointed at me. I saw it!"

"I just have to figure out who to call!" I said. Part of me definitely thought, Call Mom and Dad! You need them! But another part thought, Is there ANYONE else? Because Mom and Dad are going to KILL me!

Then I remembered—I did have the number for someone else. Someone who lived in my new neighborhood and would know about the trains to get there.

"I'm calling Charlie," I said. "Charlie's smart. He can help us."

"He hates me!" Mary Majors said.

"He doesn't hate you," I said, as Charlie's line started ringing. "He just wants you to stop being mean."

Then Charlie said, "Hello?"

"It's Celie!" I said. "You have to help us!" I told him as quickly as I could what had happened.

"I tried to warn you!" he said. "You can't let Mary Majors tell you what to do! She'll get you kidnapped!"

"I KNOW!" I said. There were BOY voices getting louder on the street—I worried that group was about to turn the corner. "You have to HURRY!" I told Charlie. "We need another A stop! NOT Jay Street-MetroTech, but near it. NOW!" Then I told him the names of the streets on the street sign from that corner.

I started pulling Mary Majors farther down the deserted street. There was an empty parking lot on our right now, and a boarded-up building on our left.

"This isn't fun at all," Mary Majors said. She kept looking over her shoulder. And she sounded like she might cry.

"OF COURSE IT'S NOT FUN!" I told her.

"I'm on Google Maps," Charlie said. "I'm trying to figure it out—hold on—wait—"

Then those boys did turn the corner! One of them RACED toward us, and another RACED after him, and the second one LEAPT on the first one, and they both landed on the sidewalk near us, and then there was hitting, and the rest of their group started hollering, and I yelled at Mary Majors, "GOOOO!"

We were both running when Charlie started saying things like, "Left at the next corner. Now tell me where you are. Straight for three more blocks. Where are you?" Until we FINALLY got to another station with an A.

"Thank you, thank you, thank you," I told him.

I texted Jo to say I was on my way home, on the A.

Then I told Mary Majors, "From now on, you're calling Charlie by his name. Or 'Professor Larken.' Absolutely nothing else." Then we went into the station and got on the A.

I did NOT SPEAK to Mary Majors on that train. She'd talked me into everything, and I should've kept saying NO, but I didn't, and we could actually have ended up DEAD!

Instead of talking, I mostly stared at a list of A train stops that was posted on the wall of the train, and I kept counting how many we had left until we got home. I wanted so badly to be there—and I worried, too. I hoped I could maybe convince Jo not to tell Mom and Dad that I'd gone missing. In my head I made a list of promises that might work. Like, "I'll ALWAYS let you use our bathroom first, even if I really have to pee. Just, please, don't tell Mom and Dad."

I never had a chance to even try to persuade Jo, though. Because when we finally got off the train, Jo AND Mom AND Dad—and Charlie and both

of his parents!—were all at the station entrance,
waiting and watching for us.

"I'm going to KILL you!" Jo shouted, as soon as she
saw me. Then she was hugging me, and my parents
were hugging me, and we were all crying. And
Charlie's parents were saying things like, "I'm so glad
they're safe!"

We left the station together. They asked lots of
questions about what had happened. And Charlie
actually tried to apologize to me and Mary Majors.

"Sorry my parents are here," he said. "It's just—I
couldn't sit at home, not knowing if you'd made
it. I HAD to come here and wait. But when I told
my parents I had to go to the subway station for a
while, they made me explain. Then they said they
had to come, too, so they could help, if you ended
up needing it. That's just the way they are."

He truly looked sorry.

"You are NOT ALLOWED to apologize about anything!" I told him. "You saved us!"

I expected Mary Majors to say something like, "You really did." But she was watching both sets of parents, who at that point were walking a tiny bit ahead, with Jo. And she was very, very quiet.

I got even MADDER at her then. Because she should've thanked Charlie!

I didn't say anything, though, because Charlie's parents turned back to us and said they'd walk Mary Majors to her apartment. And we all split up.

Jo did NOT apologize for meeting me with Mom and Dad. "You scared me so badly, when you didn't answer my calls or texts!" she said, as we walked home. "I kept trying and trying!" She'd finally gone to get Mom and Dad in the movie theater, to tell them I wasn't answering. There's no reception in the theater—that's why my calls to her hadn't gone through. They'd all seen my last text, though. The one that said I was getting on the A and coming home.

Of course they all wanted to know where I'd been. And when I said, "At Violet's," they all started talking at once. "You went all the way to VIOLET'S?" Mom said, and Dad said, "How did you get there?" and Jo said, "Did you see Jake?"

So I told Jo quickly, "Jake's working with Trina's brother on a song for you. Trina's brother writes songs. That's why Jake's being weird."

"Ohhhh," Jo said. And she seemed happy, which made me happy.

But my parents had lots of questions about how I'd gotten to Violet's, and why I hadn't called them for permission, and how I'd gotten back, and why I hadn't called them for help before getting on the subway alone. Those questions did not make me happy. And my answers did not make them happy.

Dad got stuck for a while on the subject of Shayna. He kept saying things like, "She just left you there? Two ten-year-olds, by yourselves, so far from home and with no way to get back? Are you sure?"

"Yes," I told him. "I am one hundred percent sure."

As soon as we walked in our apartment, Mom and Dad said they wanted to talk to me alone in my room. That was NOT a good conversation. They talked a lot about having trust, then breaking it. I definitely started to cry.

Finally my dad said, "Trust can also be rebuilt." And my mom said, "Let's focus on rebuilding." And I said, "Yes, please."

"You'll have to start rebuilding right here," Dad said. "Because you're not going anywhere except school and home for the next three weeks."

Mom looked at him and nodded, and I could see they were making up my punishments right then.

"You'll do plenty of chores, too," she said. "And no shows on the computer or TV."

"No cell phone, either, for those weeks," Dad said, holding out his hand for it.

That last one was the worst! I didn't care about staying home—I didn't want to go anywhere else. Chores were fine—I deserved them—and I could do without shows. But how could I make up with Violet if I couldn't text her? How could I keep in touch with Lula, too? I'd have no friends here— except for Charlie—AND no friends there. No friends anywhere at all.

I knew I couldn't fight with my dad. So I took my phone out of my pocket and handed it to him. But I also said, "Remember, this phone saved me. I wouldn't have been able to call Charlie without it."

"We wish you'd also used it to call us," Mom said.

"That's exactly what I'll do from now on, I

promise," I said. "But I can't call you if I don't have the phone."

"We'll think about that," my dad said. He did not hand me back my phone. Instead, he said, "When was the last time you ate?"

"Breakfast," I said. And I realized how hungry I was. I'd been so distracted, I hadn't even noticed.

Mom and Dad made me a big bowl of pasta then, and they sat with me while I ate. After that they sent me to my room, as the start of my three weeks of punishment. And I've been in here ever since.

I am so very, very tired.

## After a snooze

I just fell asleep for a while and drooled all over my pillow. Jo woke me up. "Mom and Dad wouldn't let me in until now!" she said. "You have to tell me everything—every single detail. I called Jake and talked to Violet, too, so I know a lot. But I want to hear the whole story from you, from the very beginning."

I was half-asleep until she said she'd talked to Jake and Violet. That woke me all the way up.

"Do they both hate me?" I asked her.

I never thought I'd have to ask that. I hated having to ask it.

"Jake's just annoyed with you," Jo said. "He hates Mary Majors. Violet's pretty mad at you. But we'll talk about that when we get there. You have to start at the very beginning of the day."

So we sat side by side on my bed, and I started at the very beginning. It wasn't easy to tell her every detail. Because there was plenty for her to be mad about. She was NOT happy that I'd told Mary Majors all about her Jake problems, for example. Or that we'd invaded his room and fought with him while he was in a towel. But I knew she wasn't a hundred percent angry about that. Because she was also very, very glad to have found out that Jake was writing her a song. And not cheating on her with Mean-a Trina.

Still, she was firm with me about one thing. She turned to face me on the bed and said, very seriously, "You should never have let that Mary Majors girl convince you to go all the way to Jake and Violet's without telling us. It was so scary when I didn't know where you were, and you could've been anywhere—you could actually have been kidnapped—and I had no way to know, or to help you. You can't EVER do that again." By the time she'd finished that speech, she looked like she was about to cry.

"I won't do it again," I told her.

"Do you solemnly swear?" she said.

"I solemnly swear," I said.

"And do you solemnly swear to never confront

Jake again without talking to me first? And doing exactly what I say?" she said.

"Yes," I said. "I solemnly swear."

"Good," she said. She rested her head on my shoulder, and we sat there very quietly for a little bit. Then she hopped off my bed and said, "Time to watch a movie."

"That's not nice!" I said. Because Mom and Dad were definitely not going to let me watch a movie.

"Oh!" she said quickly, realizing what I meant. Then she thought for a second and said, "It's educational—for school—very boring."

That made me laugh a little. She was so obviously lying. But at least she was trying.

"Just go," I told her, pointing at my door.

She grinned at me and left.

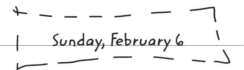

Today I did SO MANY CHORES! For starters, I washed and dried and folded FOUR LOADS of laundry. I think my parents FAKED laundry, to torture me!

They SAY we're dirty...

...but we're actually sparkly clean!

I loaded and unloaded the dishwasher, too. Twice! And Mom made me take the last of our unopened boxes out of the closet in her office and put EVERYTHING away.

The only good thing about today: I got to spend lots of time with Granny. She sat in the kitchen with Eye-Della, and we all talked while I loaded and unloaded the dishwasher. Plus I took clean laundry to the den and folded it in there, with the two of them.

"She's such a sweet girl, isn't she?" Granny said a lot, to Eye-Della.

"Yes, she sure is sweet," Eye-Della said to Granny. Even though she must've figured out that I was doing all that housework because I'm being punished for doing something bad. She smiled and told me, "This too shall pass," when I started loading dishes AGAIN.

I'm glad I don't have to rebuild with Granny and Eye-Della, at least.

Also, in my little breaks from chores, I started trying to make up with Violet. Jo let me borrow her phone, and I sent her texts like these:

"I didn't know Mary Majors had that plan! REALLY!"

and

"I would've stayed FAR from Jake's room, if it wasn't for her. obviously! he was wearing a TOWEL!"

and

"would it help if I wrote you a love song?"

So far, no response from Violet.

I asked Jo if we could leave for school early today. Because I'm already tired of being stuck at home! She said yes, which was nice of her. And I was the first kid in our classroom.

Very surprisingly, Mary Majors came in second. And she wasn't even out of breath—I think she just left her apartment with plenty of time to get to school, for once. I was already at my desk, taking a notebook and pen out of my backpack. She walked over to me, and I thought, Do NOT ask me to do anything with you. Because I am NOT going to do it.

She didn't ask me to do something, though. Instead, she asked, "Are your parents really mad?"

I nodded and said, "I'm very punished, for three weeks. How about you?"

She shrugged and said, "Nobody even cared that I'd been gone."

Which seemed weird. And sad!

I don't want to be punished. (Last night Mom said she's going to teach me how to mop! I don't want to know how to mop!) But still. I'm glad my family cared that I was gone.

I was still at my desk with Mary Majors when Charlie walked in. I got ready to yell at her then, if I needed to. If she was mean to him for even one second. But she just said, "Hi, CHARLIE." Emphasizing his name. And also, "Thanks for helping us the other day."

I couldn't get mad at that.

Plus, when Josie came in a little later and said to Charlie, "How's it going, Spot?" Mary Majors said, very loudly, "That's NOT FUNNY, Josie."

I couldn't get mad at that, either.

I still don't think I ever want to do anything with Mary Majors outside of school again. Or maybe even outside the classroom. And I'm still mad at her for lots of things. Like wrecking my friendship with Violet. But I have to admit, she's trying.

## Later, At Home, After taking our trash Down to the Basement

Charlie's mom just called my mom, to see how we were all doing. After they talked, Mom and Dad decided that Charlie could come home with me after school tomorrow. Since he's my homework buddy.

I'm super happy about that. Except, Mom says that as soon as our homework is done, I have to do my chores. So I hope Charlie doesn't mind watching while I clean the kitchen.

Isn't this so much fun?

Charlie is excellent at washing dishes! He says
he LIKES doing it! It's a little odd. But extremely
helpful! He rinsed dishes, and I loaded the
dishwasher, and we figured out a list of texts to try
to make Violet like me again. Here's the one I just
sent her, on Jo's phone:

i hate that you're mad at me even more than i hate
medians and modes. and those things are the worst. ☹

I wanted to send a text promising I'd never speak
to Mary Majors again if Violet forgave me. But
Charlie wouldn't let me. Because she really is trying
hard. Today she saved me and Charlie a seat at her
table at lunch. We told her, "No, thanks." Because
kids who'd been mean to Charlie, like Josie, were
sitting there. Mary Majors could've just nodded
and said, "Okay." But instead she stood up with her
lunch and came and sat with us.

She's making it hard to stay super angry at her. But
I'd still stop talking to her if Violet asked me to.

# After Charlie Left

Dad gave me back my cell phone! Only for emergency situations, though. I can't use it for any other reason, for the rest of my three punishment weeks.

I asked whether I could text Violet. Since our problems definitely count as an emergency. But Dad said, "That's not the kind of emergency I mean."

I feel very limited.

Even so, I'm very glad to have this beautiful phone back.

## A Little Later

I just checked with Jo. Still no reply from Violet.

Feeling as sad as a celery stick.

## Even Later

I started feeling desperate about the Violet situation. I couldn't think what to do. Finally I wrote this poem and texted it to her on Jo's phone:

Roses are boring.
VIOLETS are the greatest.
I can't care about sugar right now.
You being mad at me
is what I hate-est.

Jo took a look at the poem and shook her head. But

that desperate thing worked! Violet FINALLY wrote back! And we texted! This is what we said:

**Violet:** you are a terrible poet.

**Me:** sorry about that! and I am so, so sorry that I came over there with Mary Majors. I should've just come by myself, and done nothing but hang out with you.

**Violet:** Jake's been talking to Jo. he thinks I should forgive you, but not Maniac Mary Minors.

**Me:** please thank him for me. and tell him I'm so, so sorry, too.

**Violet:** ok. gotta go now.

**Me:** I'll text again soon.

That was it. She didn't call me Celie♥. Or say anything like, "I ♥ Celie♥." But at least those texts are progress.

**Wednesday, February 9**

I had a good day today. Even though Mom made me organize the pantry after I'd finished my homework. (We had a jar of olives in there that expired three years ago! WHY DID WE BRING THEM WITH US WHEN WE MOVED?)

I am as old as the hills.

My walk home from school with Jo was especially nice. She said Jake had told Violet that she should come with him when he visits Jo on Sunday. So she can talk to me in person. I hope she comes! I know we can work things out, if we get some time together.

Maybe I could convince Mom and Dad to let us go to that nice bakery with Jake and Jo. Or maybe we'll have to stay home, and she'll have to watch me fold our laundry. Either way, somehow, I'll make it okay.

170

One funny thing happened, as I was walking with Jo. We passed the A train station in our neighborhood. It is definitely NOT a nice station. The paint is peeling down there, and it's shadowy, and the trash cans are overflowing, and it smells funny. But still. As we were passing it, I remembered everyone waiting there for me, so worried, when I was finally getting back from Violet's. I remembered what it felt like to see them watching for me as I walked up the stairs from the train. And I got such a nice feeling.

I guess Jo was thinking exactly the same thing. Because she pointed at the sign for the station and said to me, "I somehow love that place."

"Me too," I said. "It weirdly reminds me of home."

# Check out Celie's last two adventures!

Ten-year-old Celie turns to her brand-new diary as she tries to sort through everything on her mind: fights with her sister, Jo, an increasingly forgetful grandmother, and worst of all, a best friend who won't speak to her!

★ "Sternberg gets Celie's voice just right, and readers should find her completely credible. . . . This satisfying slice-of-life story about the permutations of friendship and family resonates." —*Kirkus Reviews*, starred review

"Sternberg exposes the travails of adolescence with authenticity and humor." —*Publishers Weekly*

"A promising new family-and-friendship series grounded by a likable, authentic protagonist." —*Booklist*

HC: 978-1-59078-993-3 • $15.95 U.S. / $19.99 CAN
PB: 978-1-62979-405-1 • $6.95 U.S. / $8.50 CAN
e-book: 978-1-62979-284-2 • $7.99

THE TOP-SECRET DIARY OF CELIE VALENTINE

Secrets Out!

Julie Sternberg
illustrated by Johanna Wright

Celie once again fills her diary as she faces some big life changes, such as her grandmother moving in, her parents keeping secrets, her sister going boy crazy, and her best friend drifting away.

"Although the issues Celie faces—loss of her best friend, conflicts with her sister, concerns about her cognitively compromised grandmother—are major, the story is in no way heavy . . . A heartfelt but amusing story about the many challenges of growing up." —*Kirkus Reviews*

"Celie's voice is fresh, completely unselfconscious, and emphatic . . . Much of the book's considerable humor, as well as its pathos, is communicated in Celie's sketches, diagrams, and notes—scribbly, heartfelt, and immediate." —*Horn Book*

HC: 978-1-62091-777-0 • $15.95 U.S. / $19.99 CAN
e-book: 978-1-62979-434-1 • $7.99